PRINCE ON A

He urged the horse on. It was very richly decked out in white and gold, and so was he, which surprised him.

"But then," he reasoned, "I am a Prince. Am I? It's a pity," he said to the horse, "you can't tell me what all this is about – if only I could remember." He was really talking to keep his courage up, because he was certain he could now see shadowy figures and red eyes glinting in the darkness. "It must be a spell, or perhaps a blow on the head – that thing when you forget everything — amsneezia, is it?"

"Amnesia," said the horse.

"Then you *can* talk!" cried the Prince delightedly.

"Of course I can't," said the horse. "Whoever heard of a horse talking?"

Also available in Beaver by Tanith Lee

East of Midnight
Companions on the Road
The Winter Players
The Dragon Hoard

PRINCE ON A WHITE HORSE

Tanith Lee

Beaver Books

A Beaver Book

Published by Arrow Books Limited
62-65 Chandos Place, London WC2N 4NW

An imprint of Century Hutchinson Limited

London Melbourne Sydney Auckland
Johannesburg and agencies throughout the world

First published by Macmillan Children's Books 1982
Beaver edition 1989

© Tanith Lee 1982

Made and printed in Great Britain
by Courier International Ltd
Tiptree, Essex

ISBN 0 09 957150 1

Contents

CHAPTER ONE

The Waste

The Prince had been riding a featureless track over the dry and empty waste for ten hours. A cold wind was blowing through the rocks, and snapping nastily at the occasional leafless tree, of which there weren't many. The Prince didn't know who he was or how he had got here. He had been puzzling over it for several minutes now, and once he had thought of an acorn, but that hadn't made sense, and he had forgotten it again. Apart from this, he could make out only that he was a prince – though who? – that he was riding a white horse – though whose? – and that they had been going through this waste for ten hours – though why? Perhaps he was here on a holiday.

"And I don't even know my name," grumbled the Prince. "Could it be Richard? Or *Cecil?*"

It was getting dusky and cold, and the Prince – Alexander? Cuthbert? – stared up at some dark unfriendly-looking mountains in front of him on the horizon.

"Now is that East or West? Or North?" worried the Prince. "If only I had a compass. Perhaps I have." After rummaging for a moment, he decided he hadn't. He leaned over and looked at the horse. "Excuse me, horse, but can you tell me why I'm here, and who I am, and where this is?"

But the horse couldn't, or wouldn't. It stared up at the mountains and flared its nostrils.

"Or South?" added the Prince.

Just then there was a kind of whirling in the air in front of them, and after a moment a girl stood on the track. She wore a scarlet dress with a golden girdle, and every strand of her long black hair sparkled with bits of gold shaped like little beetles.

"Who are you, and whom do you seek?" cried the girl.

"I don't know," said the Prince, admiring her grammar.

The girl blinked, but she went on determinedly, "Ahead lies the Castle of Bone, guarded by the Dragon of Brass. All the secrets of the world are hidden there, but all who seek them perish in the Dragon's jaws."

"Well, in that case," said the Prince, "I think I'll leave it."

The girl blinked again, and frowned, and said sternly, "Then, if I cannot dissuade you, take this magic sword."

There was another whirling in the air, and out of it the girl snatched a sword of white metal, set with rubies at the hilt, and thrust it on the Prince.

"Thank you," said the Prince. "Who are you?" he added.

The girl smiled. He had obviously said the right thing at last.

"I am Gemael the Red, brave prince, the Lady of the Waste."

"Do you happen to know who *I* am?" asked the Prince.

The girl stamped her foot, pointed at the mountains, hissed "Godspeed" in a cross voice, and disappeared again.

"Well, it certainly isn't a holiday," said the Prince.

The sky was by now a dark and murky blue, and the mountains stood out black against it in sharp, dangerous shapes. Half way up one of the nearest the Prince could now make out a weird shifting light, which he didn't like the look of one bit.

"That must be something to do with the Castle of Bone," said the Prince. "Or the Dragon. Well, I don't have to go there," he told himself, and yet he had the most unpleasant feeling that he did have to. "Well, I'll make camp here for the night, and worry about it in the morning."

But just then he noticed that the air around him felt very prickly and strange, and the wind seemed full of squawks and squeals and howls, and the darker it got the louder they got, and some of the rocks seemed oddly luminous, and he didn't think, really, he wanted to stay here after all.

He urged the horse on. It was very richly decked out in white and gold, and so was he, which surprised him.

"But then," he reasoned, "I am a Prince. Am I? It's a pity," he said to the horse, "you can't tell me what all this is about – if only I could remember." He was really talking to keep his courage up, because he was certain he could now see shadowy figures and red eyes glinting in the darkness. "It must be a spell, or perhaps a blow on the head – that thing when you forget everything – amsneezia, is it?"

"Amnesia," said the horse.

"Then you *can* talk!" cried the Prince delightedly.

"Of course I can't," said the horse. "Whoever heard of a horse talking?"

"Oh," said the Prince.

They hurried on, and the track was much steeper now, and the mountains loomed close.

Presently the Prince thought of something.

"But you just did."

"No," said the horse.

"But you did talk – there, you did it again."

"You imagined it," said the horse.

Just then a ghastly white lightning opened the sky. The horse reared, and apologised. In the lightning, which seemed to last a long time, the Prince saw the outline of a huge white castle on the mountain slope above, with a black causeway curling round the rocks right up to its gaping doormouth. A cold glow slid from every chink of it, and it seemed to be built entirely of the bones of colossal ancient monsters. When the lightning went out, the glow went on, and staring at the bone towers and ribcage walls and vertebrae palisades, the Prince was sure he didn't want to go anywhere near it.

"Now what do I do?" cried the Prince in despair. Horrible shapes quivered all round him, and the only refuge seemed to be the awful castle.

"Draw a Bezzlegram," said the horse.

"You spoke!"

"I didn't," said the horse.

"What's a Bezzlegram?"

"It's a circle with a seven-pointed star in it and drawings of safe signs in between the points. It keeps Bezzles out."

"What are Bezzles? And I can't! And does it matter?"

"Yes," said the horse. "The things you can see all around you are Bezzles. They're demons of the

10

Waste, and they'll attack any minute unless you're inside a Bezzlegram."

"Well, I'm not and I won't be," cried the Prince in a panic.

The horse proceeded to draw a Bezzlegram in the dry ground with its hoof. It looked just the way it had said it would, a circle with a seven-pointed star inside. The 'safe signs' were a dot, a cross, a square, an oblong, a thing like the letter T, a thing like an H, and a thing that didn't look like anything at all.

"What's that?" asked the Prince, pointing at this thing.

"I don't know. I couldn't remember the last safe sign," said the horse unworriedly, going and standing in the centre of the star. "This Bezzlegram's a bit messy really altogether, but it'll keep those Bezzles out anyway. They're very ignorant. Beezles, now, or Buzzles, they're much harder to fool."

The Prince soon realised the horse must be right, because the awful cries and howls had died down to a whispering and wailing, which still made his hair stand on end, but didn't seem so close. After a time, when it got completely dark, the Prince could make out a ring of eyes all round the Bezzlegram, but they were a safe three or four yards away. He didn't like them much, even so.

"Will they go away again at daybreak?" he asked the horse, finally getting off its back.

"Oh yes, or the moonlight might drive them off."

"Ah. When does the moon rise?"

"Which one?"

"How do you mean?" asked the Prince. "You know, the moon, that round white thing."

"*Which* moon, I meant. There are three, and none of them is round."

"They must be," said the Prince.

But he was wrong. Just at that moment one of the moons appeared over the mountains, and it was an almost perfect square.

"That's silly," said the Prince. "It can't be that shape."

He said this again, later on, when the other two rose. One of them was an oval, and the other was a heart.

"It's obvious to me," said the horse, sitting beside him in the Bezzlegram (the moonlight hadn't driven the Bezzles off), "that you come from quite a different country."

The Prince put out his hands to the small fire he hadn't been able to light, recollected, shivered, put them back and said, "If only I could *remember* where I came from."

"Well, you do," said the horse. "At least you remember things like a round moon. How daft that must look."

"That's different," said the Prince. "Well, at least tell me," he added, "how I got to be sitting on your back."

"I can't *tell* you anything," said the horse with dignity.

"Oh, very well. How did I get on to your back?"

"You were just there," said the horse.

"What, out of nowhere?"

"Precisely," said the horse.

"That's silly," said the Prince, but he caught sight of the three moons again, and he thought perhaps it wasn't so silly hereabouts.

"Didn't you mind?" he tried.

"No," said the horse. "When you arrived I suddenly had all these white and gold trappings. I don't mind people dropping in when they bring presents."

"Before I came," said the Prince, "what were you doing?"

"Being a lion," said the horse.

The Prince was interested despite himself.

"Can you change at will?"

"Always. Everyone can."

"*I* can't," said the Prince.

"You haven't tried," said the horse.

But when the Prince tried, he still couldn't. He went on being a Prince, instead of a tiger or a wolf or an ostrich and all the other things he had tried to be.

"It's because you come from another country, I expect," said the horse consolingly.

The Prince thought a moment. A cunning look crossed his face.

"If I come from another country," he said, "which country is this?"

"It's simply here," said the horse.

"Hasn't it a name?"

"Oh no," said the horse disdainfully.

"Well, it's like being in the back of beyond, if you ask me," grumbled the Prince.

"Whose back?" enquired the horse gently. "And if

it were, wouldn't you be *on* it, not *in* it?"

Despondently the Prince rolled himself in his cloak and lay down to sleep. The ten hours' riding he knew he had put in had tired him out, not to mention Gemael the Red, the castle, the Bezzles and the horse. Despite the cold he grew drowsier and drowsier. The very last thing he saw as his eyes closed was a silver chariot, shaped like an open flower, being pulled over the sky by three silver horses with fiery wings.

"That's pretty," he murmured, and fell asleep.

CHAPTER TWO

The Castle of Bone

"A silver chariot shaped like an open flower, being pulled over the sky by three silver horses with fiery wings!" cried the Prince, sitting up with a terrific start. "That's silly! Oh, no it isn't. I forgot."

It was dawn and the sky was gold, with clouds like huge red roses floating about in it. The Prince nervously stared to make sure they weren't actually roses, but they were clouds all right. A big lion was sitting a few yards away, outside the Bezzlegram, washing its paws.

The Prince was rather scared, wondering if it might be hungry.

"Good morning," he said very politely. "Do you speak too?"

"No," said the lion.

"Ah–ha," said the Prince. "It's you. You're being a lion again."

"I'll be a horse when you want to ride me," said the lion.

The Prince stretched, wondering why he felt so well and cheerful when he was in such a ridiculous place, and didn't know the first thing about himself.

"I see the Bezzles have gone."

"Mostly," said the horse-lion. "I had one for breakfast."

The Prince didn't like to think about this.

"Did you see the silver flower chariot?" he asked quickly.

"Yes. It's one of the chariots of the Sky People."

At that moment the sun rose over the Waste, and the Prince was certain, before it became too bright to look at, that the sun had a hole in the middle just like a doughnut. He decided not to mention it.

"What do we do now?" he asked the horse-lion.

"I thought you wanted to go to the Castle of Bone."

"Not really, I just felt I had to. I still do, in fact," added the Prince gloomily.

"Well, it's quite safe by day," said the horse-lion, giving itself a shake and turning back into a horse. "Look."

The Prince did look, and the castle still seemed ancient and peculiar, but the bones were lacquered golden by the sun, and the cold light was gone from the windows.

"Right," said the Prince bravely, and swung himself into the saddle.

The horse started forward at a brisk trot. They crossed the rocks and were soon on the smooth causeway, riding upwards. In spite of his cheerful mood, the Prince couldn't help noticing the bones lying about by the side of the road, and the broken-off swords and crushed helmets rusting in little piles.

"Would that be the Dragon of Brass, do you suppose?"

"Who else?" said the horse.

After travelling for about half an hour, they reached the huge doorway, filled by a massive black door with brazen studs. The Prince felt he ought to knock on the door with the hilt of the sword Gemael the Red had given him. When he did so, a great clanging boomed and echoed through the castle.

For a long while nothing happened, except that the echoes died away. And then there came the sound of heavy footsteps on bone floors, and a chink of metal.

The Prince got nervous.

"I've changed my mind," he said urgently. "Can we ride away rather fast – or could you draw another Bezzlegram or something?"

"I don't think it would be any good," said the horse. "That sounds more like a Beezle to me."

Just then there came the scream of a key in the lock, and the door was flung open.

Framed in the doorway stood a gigantic muscular creature, covered from neck to knees in a sort of furry tunic, with a brass studded belt at its waist. Arms, legs and a head just as furry as the tunic protruded through holes; but the tunic fur was white and the rest black. Long yellow eyes and teeth glittered in the fur. A single horn stuck out where its nose should have been, and a club was thrust through its belt. In one taloned paw it carried an enormous key-ring, in the other a mop and bucket.

"*Is* it a Beezle?" whispered the Prince anxiously.

"No, a Buzzle," said the horse.

"That's worse isn't it—" began the Prince, but was interrupted by the Buzzle, which roared out, "WHAT DO YOU WANT?" At which the causeway trembled, as if in an earthquake, from the noise, and the Prince almost fell down.

"Is this— is this— the Castle of Bone— wh-where all the secrets of the w-w-world are hidden?" he got out at last.

"YES," thundered the Buzzle, though more quietly. "WHAT ABOUT IT?"

"Well, can I come in?"

"I DON'T SEE WHY NOT," shouted the Buzzle, "AS LONG AS YOU WATCH OUT AND DON'T DIRTY MY FLOORS."

It waved them in and shut the door with a terrible bang.

"I— er— won't have to fight the Dragon of Brass, will I?" asked the Prince.

"NO. THAT'S ONLY AT NIGHT."

Having got them inside, and decided they were "VISITORS", the Buzzle became quite jolly, and took them into its "ROOM". It said it was the caretaker of the castle, and offered the Prince breakfast. The Prince gladly accepted, but it turned out that the Buzzle thought raw eggs and watercress were what he wanted (which they weren't). The Prince managed to tip them out of a window when the Buzzle wasn't looking.

"YOU SEE," screamed the Buzzle, as it took them on a guided tour of the castle some twenty minutes later, "IT'S QUITE NICE FOR ME TO MEET SOMEBODY FROM OUTSIDE, AND YOU A PRINCE AND ALL."

"And the horse," put in the Prince politely.

"OH, HORSES AREN'T ANY GOOD. YOU CAN'T TALK TO A HORSE."

"Quite right," said the horse approvingly.

"But if the castle's safe by day, don't you ever get anyone calling here then?" asked the Prince.

"NOBODY EVER GETS HERE BY DAY," yelled the Buzzle, "ONLY BY NIGHT."

"Always?"

"ALWAYS."

"But that's sill—" began the Prince and stopped.

18

"But supposing they stay in the Waste until morning?"

"THEY GET EATEN BY BEZZLES, THEY DO."

"I didn't, said the Prince.

"YOU DREW A BEZZLEGRAM."

"Oh yes. No, I didn't, the horse did."

"HORSES DON'T DRAW. YOU MUST HAVE DONE."

The Buzzle led them up many flights of bone stairs into a long bone gallery. Here were several statues in a row, all painted and dressed in beautiful clothes. The Prince thought they must be past lords and ladies of the castle, but the Buzzle said it didn't know who they were, and hurried them on. There were several other places where the Prince would have liked to stop – rooms of magnificent furniture, and caskets of jewels – but the Buzzle said they didn't want to bother with those; what it was going to show them was much more interesting. The Prince became very excited thinking it was about to reveal one or all of the hidden secrets of the world.

Eventually they came to the top of a high tower.

"THERE!" boomed the Buzzle rapturously.

The Prince looked round the room, and it was perfectly empty.

"Where, exactly?"

"THERE! THERE!" And the Buzzle ran forward and clasped something in its paws. "BEYOND PRICE. YOU MAY HOLD IT."

"Thank you," said the Prince, and took the thing. He thought it might just be invisible, but it wasn't even that. It wasn't there at all. He caught the Buzzle glaring at him, so he said, "It's really lovely. You must be very proud."

"I AM," howled the Buzzle.

"The point is," ventured the Prince, "I was hoping to see some of the hidden secrets of the world."

"OH, YOU WON'T SEE THOSE IN THE DAYTIME. THEY'RE ONLY HERE AT NIGHT, ALONG WITH ALL THE FRIGHTFUL THINGS."

The Prince felt very dismayed, because he had begun to realise that what he probably had to do at the castle was to see these secrets of the world, and now he would have to spend a night here, after all.

"Is that when the Dragon's about?" he asked.

"YES. NOT TO MENTION THE SKOLKS AND OGGRINGS. I ALWAYS HIDE, BUT THEY DON'T HALF MAKE A MESS OF THE PLACE – AND ALL THOSE BONES AND BITS OF ARMOUR LEFT LYING AROUND JUST ANYWHERE—"

"This is awful!" lamented the Prince. "I do so want to run away, and I don't seem able to."

Remembering the mess the Skolks and Oggrings made, however, the Buzzle suddenly became very efficient, and hurried off to mop and dust everything. The Prince sat on the floor with his head in his hands.

"Whatever shall I do?"

A kind of whirling began to happen in the air. After a moment or so, a girl in a red dress appeared in the centre of the room.

"Who are you?" she cried. "And whom do you seek?" And then, "Oh, it's still you. Have you killed the Dragon yet, oh brave Prince?"

"No," said the Prince.

Gemael the Red looked surprised and annoyed.

"I gave you the magic sword," she shouted, and the sword rattled on its own in the Prince's scabbard. "Use it on the Dragon tonight, or you will rue the day we met. Godspeed," she finished, and whirled herself away.

The day went by very quickly as the Prince wandered worriedly about the splendid rooms of the castle. By the time sunset showed in the windows he was very hungry and very, very frightened. The horse had turned into a lion again in the afternoon, and gone off somewhere. The Prince thought it would probably go back into the Waste, and draw a Bezzlegram, and stay there all night if it had any sense.

The majestic shadows lengthened in the rooms, and some stars sneaked out over the Waste. The Prince ran up and down the stairs, looking for the Buzzle. Finally he found it hastily locking doors with its key-ring.

"Almost time, then?" said the Prince unhappily.

"CAN'T STOP NOW," yodelled the Buzzle, and ran past him down the corridor. The Prince ran after it. "HAVE TO LOCK UP THE VALUABLES, AND THEN I GO AND HIDE IN MY ROOM."

Just then they reached the "ROOM". The buzzle dived inside, and suddenly there was only a blank wall with no door in it at all.

"A friend in need is a friend indeed," said the Prince sourly.

At that instant, the last purple glimmer faded from the sky. It grew very quiet and dark, and then an icy wind came rushing from nowhere, sweeping like a great cold broom through every crevice of the Castle of Bone. The Prince shuddered, and pressed himself back against the wall to let it past, because he felt the wind knew he was there, and would be angry if he didn't show it proper respect. After the wind, he began to hear a lot of strange noises, a sort of creaking and groaning like a forest of old trees, and he didn't like it at all.

"I must try to find a candle or something, now it's got so dark," he muttered and, squaring his shoulders, and putting one hand on the hilt of Gemael's sword, he went back up the corridor in the direction of a big hall he thought he remembered seeing earlier.

It was now as black as the bottom of a tar barrel. The Prince had to feel his way with his hands and stumbled over stairs and furniture all the time. He began to count his steps aloud to cheer himself up. When he reached one hundred and seventy there was a distinct echo to his words, and he thought he had got to the hall. He remembered there had been brass candle branches in the walls, each with about fourteen bone white candles apiece, and after a lot of accidents, he managed to find one and get it down. Then he recalled he had nothing to light it with. He was standing there, feeling stupid, when he realised there *was* a light in the hall, and it was gliding towards him.

"Get back!" cried the Prince hoarsely, drawing his sword. But the light took no notice, and floated nearer. What was more, it made a peculiar noise at him. "Go away!" yelled the Prince. "Beware of my sword!" The light didn't.

The Prince broke into terrified flight. He fell over hundreds of things, and candles rained from the candlebranch, and all the while the light clattered after him, making the most horrible sounds. Finally, the Prince hit his head on something, and sat down abruptly on the floor. The awful creature rushed up, stamped on his sword arm, just as he was trying to use it, and lit the three candles left in the candle-branch.

The Prince found he was staring up at the horse, which held a lighted taper in its mouth, and had therefore been unable to speak properly. The Prince removed the taper, and the horse said, "Fire is an important protection against the dark powers of the castle. The Buzzle lent me a flint, but it took ages to make it strike."

The Prince looked round the hall, and it was vast and shadowy. He had hit his head on a huge carved chair with a canopy, and spilled candles lay everywhere.

"What do I have to do?" asked the Prince. He had come to rely upon the horse, and was very glad it was here.

"I think you should draw a Draxagram on the floor, and get inside it," said the horse. "Then, with the help of the four elements, you'll be as safe as you can hope to be. Do you have any chalk?"

"No, I don't. What four elements? And what's a Draxagram?" enquired the Prince, feeling happier already.

"A stick of charcoal would do," said the horse. It turned abruptly and gave the chair a dreadful kick. One leg collapsed at once. The horse picked it up, held it awhile in the candle flame, and then proceeded to draw on the floor with the charred end. The Draxagram seemed to be a collection of eight circles, each one with bits overlapping into the other seven, which should have been impossible. When it was done, the horse shook some earth out of its hoof into a small pile inside the Draxagram, spat on it (the Prince hadn't realised horses could spit), breathed on it, and then rested the burning taper on the top.

Just as it finished, a dull ominous booming sounded from somewhere above, the doors of the hall flew open with a thud, and a great crowd of black flying things whizzed into the room. The Prince ran inside the Draxagram, still clutching the candlebranch and the sword, aware, with a cold sinking feeling, that the terrors of the night had truly begun.

CHAPTER THREE

Ysome

The Prince and the horse sat inside the Draxagram in the flickering circle of candlelight. Round and round the Draxagram on the outside beat the black flying things, glaring with unpleasant fierce eyes, and squealing with rage because they couldn't get at them.

"Are they bats?" asked the Prince.

"No," said the horse, "Oggrings."

After a time the Oggrings settled in flocks on various pieces of furniture, rustling and shrieking in the dark.

The awful booming came again from the heart of the castle.

"What now?" wondered the Prince.

Through the open door ran twenty skeletons, dressed in brazen armour and carrying great axes. They rattled and clanked across the floor and surrounded the Draxagram.

"Surrender!" cried the captain skeleton in a high whistling voice. "Come out and you will be shown mercy."

"It – er – seems like a fair offer," said the Prince.

But the skeletons shifted their axes to get a better grip, and the Oggrings rustled excitedly.

"As long as you stay in the Draxagram," said the horse, "you'll probably be safe. If you leave it, the skeletons will chop off your head and the Oggrings will eat you."

The skeletons gnashed their teeth unmusically. They lifted their axes in both hands and began to leap all round the Draxagram in a whirling circle that made the Prince feel dizzy and confused.

"Take no notice," said the horse.

But the Prince couldn't seem to take his eyes off the skeletons. Soon he began to turn round and round in circles himself, and each circle brought him a little closer to the edge.

"Join the dance," invited the captain generously.

"Why, thank you," said the Prince.

The horse got hold of his sleeve and pulled him back just in time. The Prince fell over, and the horse sat on him. The Prince struggled and complained until quite out of breath. Seeing he wouldn't get away, the skeletons stopped leaping about, and went and leaned on their axes in the shadows.

The Prince came to his senses at once, and the horse let him get up.

"The thing that bothers me," said the Prince, trying to pretend nothing had happened, "is that I shan't get to see any of the hidden secrets of the world if I'm stuck in this Draxagram all night."

"And you won't if your head's chopped off either."

Just then the darkness began to lighten.

"Is it morning already?' asked the Prince hopefully.

But it wasn't. Through the door came a troup of maidens, clad in filmy white, some carrying lanterns shining with a soft pale light, others playing little harps and pipes so that a peculiar sweet music filled the hall. At once all the skeletons froze in attitudes of fright, and, as for the Oggrings, they lifted in a frenzied cloud and fled out of a high window.

Among the maidens walked the most beautiful girl the Prince had ever seen. At least, the most beautiful he could ever remember seeing. She had long fair hair plaited with pearls, and a primrose yellow dress with a girdle of silver lilies, and she held out one hand to him, and came towards him, smiling.

"Brave Prince," cried she, "you have overcome the terrors of the Castle of Bone. I am Ysome the Saffron, the Lady of the Castle, under a spell all day, but freed by night if a brave man dares to visit me. Now, be my guest, and we will eat and drink and make merry until the stars fade, at which time I will show you all the secrets of the world which lie hidden here."

It was a very long speech to make while you were walking rather fast, and she didn't get at all out of breath, so the Prince admired her even more. He was just about to take her hand and step out of the circle, when the horse caught hold of his tunic and almost succeeded in sitting on him again.

"It's only a trick to get you to leave the Draxagram," said the horse, "because the Oggrings and skeletons have failed."

"Nonsense," said the Prince, gazing at the lovely girl, and thinking about the eating and drinking she had mentioned. "Besides, you said fire was a protection against the dark powers of the castle, and so this lady wouldn't be likely to have lamps, if she *were* a dark power."

"Those aren't flames in the lamps," said the horse, "only elflight or phosphorus."

"Oh, what's *that*?" snapped the Prince.

"To whom are you talking?" interrupted Ysome the Saffron.

"This horse – Let go!" cried the Prince.

Ysome gave a tinkling laugh.

"But, dear Prince, horses don't *talk*."

The Prince shook the horse off.

"No, they don't," he decided. And he stepped out of the Draxagram, and clasped her hand.

"Now there'll be a thunder clap, and she'll change into a monster," said the horse, but there wasn't, and she didn't. She led the Prince gently from the hall, her maidens gliding behind, swinging their lamps and playing their harps.

The horse might have thought it was mistaken, but, just as the lamp-glow was fading from the doorway, several of the skeletons sneaked out after them, grinning skull grins, and it noticed that some of the Oggrings had flown back in and were following the procession too.

The horse shook itself into a lion, picked up the taper in its mouth, and went after everybody else, with a stealthy lion tread.

Ysome the Saffron conducted the Prince through many twisting passages and up countless steps into a gigantic banqueting hall. The walls were hung with silver cobweb draperies, and bone chandeliers rattled in the ceiling lit by hundreds of luminous green beetles.

The Prince was seated at one end of the long table and helped to wonderful food on silver dishes by Ysome's maidens. She sat at the opposite end and gazed at him fondly, as he stuffed himself with roasts and pies, and drank rare wines by the jugful.

Finally he leaned back in his chair and thanked Ysome warmly.

"That's quite all right, dear Prince," said Ysome. "It was all magic food, and now you are completely in my power. I can make you do whatever I like."

And so she could. No sooner had the Prince tried to draw his sword than he found she had made him put his hand in the gravy instead, and when he tried to run at her he ran into a hanging and became completely tangled up.

"Now," said Ysome, clapping her hands (at which all her maidens turned back into the large lizards they had presumably been all the time), "I am indeed the Lady of the Castle, and I could have you killed at once, and in lots of revolting ways, but I don't think that would be so much fun as letting you get away – no, don't thank me, I haven't finished yet – and then letting the Skolks and Oggrings hunt you down."

The Prince became aware that the Oggrings had flown in at the doors and windows and were perched on the chandeliers, occasionally eating the beetles. Two skeletons dragged him roughly from the cobweb.

"Be careful not to damage him!" screamed Ysome angrily, and they cowered, and dusted him down. "Now, when I give the signal, oh Prince, you may start to run away. You can go anywhere you like, and hide anywhere you think you might enjoy, but the Skolks will find you, you can be sure. Come, my Skolks."

And through the door slunk ten hideous animals, rather like enormous jackals, with big blazing eyes and evil teeth. They stared at the Prince, and snuffled towards him to get the scent, then licked their jaws and smiled.

"When I say 'go'," cried Ysome, "the Prince will

29

run out. All the rest of us will cover our eyes and count to a hundred, after which the Skolks and Oggrings may give chase. Any cheating," she added, "will be severely punished. I like to see fair play."

The Prince tried to throw a plate at her, but found he had dropped it on his foot instead.

"Cover your eyes!" shouted Ysome, and they all did. "Go!"

The Prince spun round in a panic-sticken circle, then, with a cry of angry despair, fled out of the banqueting hall, certain that all the Skolks were peeping.

He tried to count too, as he ran, and he had only reached eighty-three when he heard the first cries behind him.

"They *did* cheat," he wailed. "Oh! If only I'd listened to the horse."

He stumbled up and down stairs, leapt over thresholds into empty rooms, where things mumbled and shrieked at him, and leapt out again. He found some of the beetles had fallen on his head and so he could see where he was going by their light. Unfortunately the Skolks and Oggrings would also be able to. Every so often he was positive he felt hot breath on his heels, and could hear the flap of wings in his ears. Then he would put on an extra burst of speed.

"But it's no use," he panted, "no use at all."

Dashing round a corner, he plunged into a whirling thing which became Gemael the Red even as he collided with her.

"Who are you?" she gasped, "and whom – haven't you killed the Dragon *yet?*"

"Oh, for goodness sake," cried the Prince and rushed past her. Gemael ran after him.

"You must destroy the Dragon, and then the castle

will fall, and my sworn enemy, Ysome the Saffron, will perish. Do you hear?"

But he didn't, and fairly soon Gemael caught sight of the Skolks, and disappeared at top speed.

The Prince now realised he was going downwards, all the flights of stairs had led this way for a long time, probably because he had found it easier to run down these than up the upwards ones.

"I shall be trapped in a cellar," he shuddered, but he couldn't turn back.

And then suddenly he ran slap into a closed door. He rubbed his nose and stared at the door. It seemed to be made of ebony, and was bolted seven times and barred seven times on his side. With frenzied fingers he strained open the top bars and bolts, and pulled the middle ones, and scrabbled at the ones at the bottom, which were very stiff. Just as he got to the last one, he heard a joyful snuffling behind him, and turned round to see three of the Skolks grinning in the passage, each with an Oggring perched on its back.

"Look," said the trembling Prince, "do Skolks talk?"

"No," said the nearest one, dribbling.

"Oh good, well in that case, I hear there's a lot of treasure here, and wouldn't you like some of it – half of it – all of it, then? Just think of the meals you could buy with a whole castle full of treasure. Eat me, and I'll be gone in a flash, all over, only a memory—"

The Skolks only smiled, and began to pad forward, the Oggrings flapping over their heads.

"Shall we eat him all now?" asked a Skolk. "Or save some for later."

"All now!" squealed an Oggring. "Before the others come and want their share."

The Prince drew his sword in desperation and lunged at them, and, as he did so, another shape burst into the passageway. He thought it was a Skolk too, but it was the horse-lion.

"Jewelstar!" shouted the horse-lion, which was apparently some kind of battle-cry, and jumped on two of the Skolks.

"Jewelstar!" echoed the Prince and, finding it made him feel braver, he chopped off the head of the nearest Skolk with one blow, and clipped the wings of an Oggring which flew into his face. After that, everything seemed to blur together, and, when he next looked round him, he and the horse-lion were standing by the door with five dead Skolks and a great pile of Oggrings in the passage.

"Quickly, open the door," said the horse-lion. "There'll be worse than Skolks in a minute."

The Prince obeyed, and they dashed through it and slammed it shut behind them. Amazed, the prince heard it locking itself on the other side.

When he looked around him, he saw that they were in a great courtyard with a tall bone tower standing remotely at the far end. It was walled on the other three sides by bone palisades, and was open to the sky. Stars and the heart moon gazed back at him, and washed the court with cool light.

"Where are we now?" asked the Prince, but the useful horse-lion was scratching a weird sign on the door with its claws.

"That will stop them unbolting it," said the horse-lion, "and we're in a courtyard."

The Prince shrugged, and went round the courtyard to see if he could find a different way out. On the ground, near the right-hand wall, was the remains of an old Draxagram someone had drawn but, judging by the bits of broken sword lying round it, they hadn't stayed in theirs either.

There didn't seem to be a way out, except possibly by the tower, but he didn't like the look of it for some reason. Turning back, the Prince found a large brass bell hanging from the wall. On it was inscribed: 'I AM HERE. SOUND THIS, AND I WILL COME.'

If the Prince had stopped to think about it, he would have realised that possibly he might not want to meet whoever was there, and would come, but somehow he didn't. He just reached up and rang the bell before he could stop himself. It gave off a most terrifying clanging that bounced from wall to wall, and the horse-lion ran up to him and cried, "You shouldn't have *done* that!"

"What will happen?" trembled the Prince.

The first thing that happened was that a great black crack appeared down the whole length of the tower, and out of it billowed rusty-red smoke. It filled the court, and turned the sky and the moon the colour of blood, and it smelled of hot metal and burning oil.

The second thing that happened was that the crack split wide open so that the tower separated into two halves, and out of the middle a glittering, huge, terrible thing uncoiled itself, its metal cogs grinding together, black steam puffing from its brazen nostrils, and fire flickering behind its empty hungry eyes.

It was unmistakably the Dragon of Brass.

CHAPTER FOUR

The Dragon of Brass

"It's the dra— the dra— Oh! Can't we draw a Draxagram?" cried the Prince.

"No," said the horse-lion, "there wouldn't be any
point. As you can see, the Dragon of Brass is made of
brass. It's all machinery, and so a Draxagram
wouldn't have any power over it."

"I don't see why not!" shouted the Prince. "I think
you're being unreasonable."

The Dragon was now clear of the tower, and was
coming across the court with a slow, metal-squealing
tread. It lashed its tail, and brass plates rattled, and a
brass forked tongue flickered noisily in and out of its
hinged jaws. The red fire behind its eyes made them
glow terribly.

"Look," said the Prince as they backed away, "it's
got fire in it, so it can't be one of the dark powers –
perhaps it's friendly."

"That kind of magic doesn't make any difference to
a machine," said the horse-lion. "Besides, the fire is
its combustion—"

"Oh, these long words!" cried the Prince.

At this moment they both banged into the courtyard wall, having backed as far as they could go.

Gemael's sword suddenly rattled by itself in the
Prince's scabbard.

"Shall I – try this?" the Prince wondered, drawing

it. "She said it was magic, after all."

"You've got nothing to lose," said the horse-lion.

So, clutching the ruby hilt and feeling cold all over, the Prince took a few steps forward to meet the Dragon. The Dragon seemed delighted, and speeded up. The prince backed away again.

"It's not fair," he said to the horse, trying to press himself through the bone wall and into another part of the castle – any other part – "I thought it stayed *outside* to guard, like a— like a dog."

The Dragon now reached the wall, and so they began to back along it, which made a change, but still didn't really improve things.

"It hasn't attacked yet," whispered the Prince. "Perhaps it won't."

Just then it did. It reared up its frightful head and lunged at him. The Prince managed to jump aside, and, stung to action, brought the magic sword crashing down against the Dragon's bodywork. The sword promptly snapped in half.

"Oh, that's a lot of use!" yelled the Prince in horrified rage.

A gale of laughter floated down from the other side of the court. As he ran away from the Dragon, the Prince was able to look up and see Ysome the Saffron and her lizards, and several Skolks, skeletons and Oggrings having gleeful hysterics on top of one of the bone palisades.

"Fool, to trust the weapons of Gemael the Red!" howled Ysome.

Blindly the Prince rained another blow or two on the Dragon, and some more of the sword snapped off. He was just about to throw it away, as it slowed him down while he ran, when the smoky air began to whirl. Out of the whirling came a dim, trembling shape with long black hair. Gemael the Red looked very pale, and she cowered inside the whirling, never quite daring to form herself properly.

"A fine time to show up!" snarled the Prince. "And look at your useless sword!"

With huge fearful eyes fixed on the Dragon, Gemael gasped in a hoarse and angry voice, "Don't you know *anything*, you stupid creature. Don't hit the Dragon with the sword, *throw* it."

"Throw it where?"

"*Oh!* Down its throat, where else, you idiot!"

"She's quite right," put in the horse-lion across the court.

The Prince stopped running. He planted himself firmly, with what was left of the sword in both hands, and watched the Dragon lumbering towards him.

"I'll tell you when," hissed Gemael. The Dragon opened its jaws, and snaked its head down to them. "Now!" screamed Gemael.

The Prince threw the sword. It arched up and in, over the six inch long brass teeth, and went down the throat with a rasping, clattering sound. The Prince fell flat, and hid his face, and waited to be crunched up. As a result of this, he didn't see what happened to the Dragon. First it hesitated and looked surprised. Then it shook itself, jumped in the air, and kicked out its six legs, one after the other, and looked even more surprised. Then there was a thud inside it, as if something had exploded, a lot of white smoke came out of its joints, and bright flashes went on and off behind its eyes. It ran on the spot, ran backwards, tried to run backwards up the wall, fell down again, and finally stopped quite still. After this, it didn't move again, simply steamed gently to itself, and made soft sizzling sounds in a corner.

The Prince looked up at last.

"I think you shorted something," said the horse-lion.

"What?" asked the Prince. He was interrupted by a shrill scream from the palisade.

Ysome the Saffron, with a very white face, had lifted her arms to call down a ghastly curse on the Prince, but it was too late. The stars had begun to fade.

"Your power is gone with the night!" cried Gemael. "And now the Dragon is dead, you must leave the castle and wander homeless, as I have done all these years."

Ysome shivered again, and ran off the palisade, closely followed by lizards, skeletons, Skolks and Oggrings, all squealing and grunting.

"Brave Prince," began Gemael warmly.

"I don't see," said the Prince with dignity, "if I was supposed to *throw* the wretched sword, why you didn't tell me when you gave it to me."

"I thought you knew," said Gemael humbly.

"Well, I didn't. And, anyway, why give it to me and not to all the other poor princes who came to the castle and got eaten?"

"You were special."

"Oh, was I?" asked the Prince, thawing slightly.

"Yes," said Gemael, "though I don't know why."

And so saying, she disappeared.

"Well," said the Prince, "it's almost dawn. I shan't see any of the hidden secrets of the world *now*."

"Whatever makes you think that?" asked a voice.

A door that the Prince hadn't seen before had

opened in the far wall, and there stood a tall straight old man. At least he looked as though he ought to be old, because his hair was white and there were lines around his eyes, but really you couldn't tell for sure. Out of the white hair at his temples grew two fine curling horns, and, instead of a garment, he was covered from neck to ankles with long, well-groomed white fur.

"Come with me," he said. "I can't show you everything because not everything concerns you. But what does, I *will* show you, I promise."

"But—" said the Prince.

The horse – it was a horse again – nudged him forward.

"It's quite all right. He's a Theel. They're incapable of harming another."

"Another what?" said the Prince vaguely.

The Theel took them into a round room. How they got there the Prince couldn't quite recall. In the middle of the room was a large cup carved of bone, but when the Prince peered down into it, what he saw was a smoky shifting mist. He had a sudden feeling he wasn't going to see anything special at all.

"Of course you will," said the Theel kindly, though the Prince hadn't spoken aloud. "However, you may not understand what you see, as yet. There are a lot of secrets, and all jumbled together like that they don't seem to be anything, but if you just stand here a minute, the ones that belong to you will arrive."

At that instant, one did. Out of the mist appeared a distinct picture of the Castle of Bone itself, caught in the rays of dawn, and it was collapsing.

"Don't be afraid," said the Theel. "It won't be

dawn for a little while, and you'll be well away by then."

"But what happened?" asked the Prince. "Is there going to be an earthquake?"

"Gemael told you that once the Dragon of Brass was destroyed the castle would fall. You ended the power of the Dragon – for the time being at any rate – so the castle *will* fall."

The Prince didn't really understand this, but he was getting used to not understanding things out here.

"What about Ysome?"

But just then he saw Ysome in the bone cup. She was sitting in the Waste, wringing her hands, surrounded by a lot of grumbling Skolks and other dreadful things the Prince didn't look at too closely. He didn't feel a bit sorry for her. But he wondered about the Theel, which seemed to live in the castle too.

"Where will *you* go?" he asked.

"Where I'm needed, just as you will."

"Will I?"

Surprised, the Prince caught a sudden glimpse of a marching army, waving banners, glinting swords, and there, at the front of it, was a young man in white and gold armour with a golden helmet on his head, and the young man looked just like himself.

"Jewelstar forever! Jewelstar undaunted!" shouted the armies.

"Jewelstar?" muttered the Prince. "Where have I heard that word before? Wait a minute, the horse used it as a battle-cry when we fought the Skolks. Why did you, horse?"

"It came into my head and seemed right at the

time," said the horse.

"But where is this Jewelstar, and what is it?"

"Don't ask me," said the horse. "Not that you'd be so foolish."

But the armies seemed to know all about it, and they were yelling even harder as they faded back into the mist.

"And there's an acorn!" exclaimed the Prince. "Whatever's an acorn doing there? Or is it? Nulgrave! It's gone!" The Prince paused. "What do I mean by *Nulgrave*? It must be a sort of curse—Ah!"

What was presumably Nulgrave had appeared in the mist. The Prince drew away from the bowl, and turned pale. There was a black coiling *something* there, and the very sight of it made him feel that wherever it was he had come from, he ought to get back there very quickly, before he and the Something got any closer to each other.

At that moment the first pink jugful of dawn brimmed over the window sill and spilled on to the floor.

"You must go," said the Theel. "But no; wait one moment," and going past the Prince to the cup, he put in one hand and drew out an egg. This seemed so ridiculous that the prince laughed, though rather shakily. "Here you are," said the Theel.

The Prince took the egg, turned it over, and asked, "What do I do with it, actually?"

"In the Egg is your personal secret," said the Theel. "You can't break the shell until it's ready, but when it's time for you to know what your secret is, it will hatch out on its own. Until then, simply keep it with you. If you lose it, you may never find out, and others might discover some way to destroy the Egg – which

40

could do endless harm, particularly to yourself."

"But do you mean," said the Prince, "that when this Egg breaks open on its own, I shall remember who I am, where I came from and what I'm supposed to be doing here?"

"Yes," said the Theel.

There came an abrupt, uneasy rumbling from under their feet.

"We must go now," said the Theel.

"But what am I to do?" cried the Prince.

"What you feel you must," said the Theel. "That's the only thing to do at any time."

Having said this, he went to the window and, to the Prince's horror, stepped out.

The Prince ran to the sill and looked down to see how badly the Theel had been hurt when he hit the ground twenty feet below, but the Theel wasn't there. He was floating gently away into the Waste on a morning breeze. He smiled and raised his hand in farewell.

"Oh, this is awful!" shouted the Prince to the horse. "I'm even more confused than before. All I've got is this stupid Egg— and— and—" – the Prince went pale again – "this feeling that I've got to get on your back, and ride over those mountains towards— something I'm not sure I'm going to enjoy. When I think I thought all this might be a *holiday*!"

There was another thud in the foundations of the castle. The Prince stopped worrying about riding and eggs, and dashed down the stairs as fast as he could, the horse behind him. They burst out of a small door, and across a bone drawbridge they hadn't seen before, which led over a frightening gap between the castle mountain and the mountain behind it. Oggrings and Skolks and skeletons and others rushed by, carrying pieces of furniture and jewels from the castle and taking no notice of anything else.

Once on the other mountain, the horse and the Prince scrambled up a winding path to put as much distance between themselves and the castle as they could.

"There's the sun now," said the Prince, looking back.

A golden slice of it had slit the horizon.

Immediately the bone castle tottered, cracked, heaved and crumbled. Bone towers and halls fell inwards, bone stairways buckled, roofs crashed, and a white cloud of bone dust hid the sun.

A sound of wailing and cursing and crying came from below.

As the dust settled, various creatures came crawling out, hiding their eyes from the light. Last of all came a big furry thing in a white furry tunic. It clutched a key-ring, but, after a moment, flung it down on the ruins. Obviously there were no more rooms to lock and unlock.

"It's the poor Buzzle," said the Prince. He had forgotten about it and now wondered what it would do, as the castle had been its home as well. Then he heard its voice booming over the crowds of Ysome's minions.

"OUT OF MY WAY. NO MORE MESSY FLOORS TO CLEAR UP FROM ALL YOU MESSY MONSTERS. GET OUT OF IT! NONE OF YOUR LIP!" – shouldering a Skolk out of its path – "FREE AT LAST!" And it strode off into the Waste whistling. It seemed to understand the Skolks had no power by day.

"Well, someone's happy," said the Prince.

He felt nervous. He put the Egg in his pocket and cleared his throat.

"Over the mountains then," he said. "It's bound to be an awful journey. But at least," he comforted himself, "I've got someone to talk to."

The horse, naturally, made no reply.

CHAPTER FIVE

Vultikan's Forge

The climb over the mountains took several days, and the Prince didn't actually ride on the horse because the horse said it found it easier to climb mountains as a lion.

It wasn't so much that it was a difficult climb, just thoroughly unpleasant. The mountains were black, sharp and spiky, and there were sharp spiky winds as well. At least there weren't any Bezzles at night, though there were wolves.

Occasionally they came to a small pool with some thin bushes growing round it. On these bushes might be a blackberry or two, and this is what the Prince lived on; the horse, when it was one, tore up the scrubby grass. Once they came to a hut, and the Prince knocked on the door, but no one would let him in. Several times they passed caves with the black wolves in them who prowled round them in the dark. The wolves snarled, but said nothing. They didn't like talking to people they might be eating later.

On the third day the Prince noticed a strange muddy-red glow on the tip of the highest peak ahead.

"What's that?" he asked the horse-lion.

"I don't know," said the horse-lion.

"At one time you seemed to know everything," remarked the Prince tartly.

"At one time I did, but we're all entitled to forget, I

suppose. Besides," it added, not unkindly, "I only seemed to know everything because you knew nothing at all."

As they got nearer, the glow became brighter. At night it was like an orange star at the bottom edge of the sky. By the time they reached the mountain where it seemed to be, and stared up it, the glow was very fierce, and strange hot smells blew down to them on the wind, along with a lot of cinders.

On the sixth day they came to a steep rocky path, and began to climb it. Twilight fell, and the Prince grew uneasy.

"I think we're climbing directly towards that red glow, and we should turn back, or go sideways or something. Listen!" he added.

A dull thudding, like blows, sounded from above, and echoed away among the peaks.

"I think it's a volcano," cried the Prince, "and it's about to erupt."

"Volcanoes," said the horse-lion, "don't sing."

And the Prince realised that a loud thunderous voice had started up overhead, in time to the blows.

> "Toil! Toil!
> Furnace boil!
> Shape and hammer,
> Hew and hoil!"

"He hasn't got much of a voice," said the Prince, who was feeling angry because he didn't want to go anywhere near the singer and he was already hurrying up the rock terraces towards him. "And what does 'hoil' mean?"

"It means he's a blacksmith – a hoiler, it's called up

here. So it must be Vultikan."

"Who's Vultikan?"

"I don't know. I just thought it must be."

The singing had meanwhile got louder and louder, and, rounding a spur of rock, they came suddenly out on to a plateau. All around it lay massive furnace pits, ablaze with orange and scarlet flame, and pouring out purple smoke. In the middle stood a colossal anvil, and, hammering on it with a colossal hammer, was a gigantic figure. It wore a black tunic, leaving bare its muscle-packed arms, and ragged red hair flapped down its back.

"Ho!!" it howled, and the Prince dived behind the rocks, but it was only another part of the song.

> "—hoil and hew,
> And hammer and shape,
> To forge a sword
> None shall escape!"

And it brought the hammer down with a final ringing blow.

"Here you are," cried the smith, turning round and holding out a sword towards the place where the Prince was hiding. "Come on now. A sword forged by Vultikan the Smith, and you won't take it!"

The Prince, feeling silly as well as scared, got up and went between the fire pits.

"Are you sure it's for me?" he asked.

"Oh, it's for you all right," said Vultikan, who had a red beard and yellow eyes, and was just as awesome from the front as from behind.

"But how did you know I was coming this way?"

"Nice night," said Vultikan, obviously thinking this question totally stupid and best ignored.

46

The Prince took the sword. It had a gleaming blade and a hilt shaped like a dragon which was made of silver inlaid with gold.

"It— isn't magic, is it?" asked the Prince.

"No," said Vultikan. "It'll cut through anything, and nothing'll cut through it. Very useful you'll find it."

"When?"

"When you get down there," said Vultikan, pointing over his shoulder at the other side of the mountain.

The Prince went across the plateau and looked down. In the light of the square moon he could see sweeps of wooded country, and what looked like the thread of a river, gleaming like black glass in the distance.

"I don't expect you can wait to get down and get to grips with all those monsters, and all that bad magic," said Vultikan, throwing some metal pieces into the nearest furnace.

"Is that what's down there, then?" asked the Prince. "Because if it is, I'm going the other way."

Vultikan clearly thought this was a great joke. He roared with laughter.

"Sit down," he invited. "I've not finished your armour yet."

"I don't want any armour. I'm not going to *need* any armour. I'm going to find a nice quiet spot, and—"

The Prince was interrupted by a furious scream from across the fires. He would have recognised it anywhere as the scream of Ysome the Saffron. And sure enough, there she stood, quivering with fury in the firelight. There was a lot of dirt on her face, and all the pearls had fallen out of her hair, and her dress had been badly torn as she scrambled up the mountains. And she was quite alone.

"Were you following me all the time?" asked the Prince curiously. "I didn't even see you."

Ysome took no notice.

"Vultikan the Hoiler," cried she, pointing at him, "I am Ysome the Saffron, Lady of the Castle of Bone, and I have work for you."

"You'll have to wait your turn," said Vultikan, stirring the metal in the furnace.

"I am Ysome the Saffron, and I *command*—" Ysome broke off, seeing Vultikan didn't care. She rubbed her hands over her face, straightened her hair, and came daintily over to the Prince.

"Sir Prince, I appeal to you! We have been enemies in the past, but can I believe you ignoble enough not to aid a lady in distress?"

"You can believe it," said the Prince. "I suppose you've come to get that Dragon mended. Well, you'll have to wait until my armour's done," he finished smugly.

Ysome began to cry. She sobbed that all her Skolks had deserted her, she had no home, and no one to love her or take care of her. The Prince started to feel uncomfortable. But just as he was getting ready to ask Vultikan to see to the Dragon first, the hoiler broke into song once again and drowned Ysome's crying. Ysome stopped crying and went up to Vultikan and yelled at him, and nobody could hear what she yelled over the noise. Eventually she went and sat on the other side of the plateau with her face turned away, scowling.

The Prince fell asleep, leaning against the horse-lion.

When he woke up Ysome was on his side of the plateau again, and there were three or four wolves sitting opposite her. They had told Vultikan they'd come about a fitting for iron claws, but they were gazing at the Prince hungrily.

The reason the Prince had woken was because Vultikan had stopped singing and hammering.

"Here's the armour then," he said. And there it was.

It lay in a heap before the Prince, and it was white and gold, and on top was a golden helm.

"I saw myself in this in the cup at the Castle of Bone," said the Prince. "If I put it on, I'll end up at the head of an army going to fight something."

"That's right," said Vultikan.

"Well, then, I won't put it on. That's that."

"Doesn't he know," said Vultikan, addressing the horse-lion, "who he is?"

"No," said the horse-lion.

"He's only pretending he doesn't, so he can trick people," said Ysome.

"I'd better tell him then," said Vultikan, taking no notice of Ysome as usual.

The Prince felt anxious and rather sick. He had a feeling he didn't want to find out.

"You," said Vultikan, "are the Looked-for Deliverer."

"What?" asked the Prince. It sounded like the name of a town, or a very old book nobody ever bothered to read.

"It means," said the horse-lion, "that you're going to help everyone, and that they're expecting you."

"But— but what am I supposed to deliver everybody from?"

Vultikan folded his great arms and glared down at the Prince.

"Nulgrave," he said.

The effect was amazing. The wolves uttered yelps of fear and ran off among the rocks, Ysome clapped her hands to her ears and began to scream again, and even the fires cowered down in their pits. The Prince felt very worried, and he couldn't help remembering the black coiling *thing*. . . .

"But I don't even understand what it is."

"You'll find out," said Vultikan. "And now, take your armour and go on your way."

The Prince, however, sat on in bewilderment.

"Now," he heard Vultikan say, "about your Dragon. Where is it?"

Ysome stopped screaming.

"In the Waste."

"Well you can't expect me to mend it if you haven't brought it with you."

"But it's huge," Ysome cried. "I thought you'd come and fetch it."

"Well I won't."

Vultikan looked around, saw that the wolves were gone, and, without a second glance at Ysome, he blew out each of the fire pits in turn with a colossal breath. Then, shouldering his tools, he strode off down the mountain. His gigantic strides had soon taken him out of sight, and well out of range of Ysome's curses.

"I suppose we'd better stay here the night," said the Prince, wishing Vultikan hadn't blown out all the fires, and that Ysome would go away, and that there weren't so many wolves about – even though he couldn't see any, he could hear them howling to each other in the distance.

He looked at the horse-lion and it already appeared to be asleep. The Prince couldn't help feeling that if the horse felt that it was safe to go to sleep, it must be, so he lay down next to it and did the same.

CHAPTER SIX

The Honnerdrin

In the morning the sky was green, and Ysome was gone.

"I think," said the horse-lion, "I heard her screaming in the night. I suppose she was being carried off."

The Prince felt quite pleased until he recalled the wolves. He didn't like to think of people being eaten, even Ysome.

"It wasn't wolves, was it?" he asked.

"I don't think so," said the horse-lion. "She didn't scream hard enough for wolves."

"Perhaps it was someone she knew," said the Prince, telling himself she was probably screaming 'Hello!' at them. After all he had enough to worry him without worrying about her as well.

They had breakfast off some squashed berries they had saved from yesterday, and, carrying Vultikan's armour between them, set off down the other side of the mountain, towards the woods.

It was a steep and dangerous mountain, but after a time they found a winding track which curled all the way down to the valley below.

The doughnut sun was high in the sky when they reached the mountain's foot. Before them lay a slope of parched grass, which gradually tumbled off into pale brown, silent oak woods and shadows.

"I don't like the look of those woods," said the

Prince. Something about them made him want to shiver and, although none of the trees were dead, they didn't look as though they were alive either.

"This is where you put on your armour," said the horse-lion, becoming a horse.

"It'll be too hot to wear," said the Prince, for it felt very hot in the valley, and close, as if just before a storm.

But the horse went forward and cropped a little of the dried grass and there was a rattling noise, and suddenly all the bits of armour flew up at the Prince and clasped themselves on to him. The breast-plate clattered on to his chest, and the greaves crashed on to his legs, and the gauntlets whizzed over his hands, the sword sheathed itself with an angry rasping noise, and the helm came down on his head with a thud that almost knocked him unconscious. The Prince was terrified. It felt like suddenly being done up in a tin can.

"What? What? Help! Why did it— !" he cried, staggering after the horse.

"That's better," said the horse. "Now get up on my back."

"I can't. I'm too heavy."

"Try," said the horse.

The Prince put one foot in the stirrup, and tried. He found he wasn't too heavy. The horse began trotting towards the woods.

"I don't think—" said the Prince, but it was too late. The dark shadow of the wood fell over him, and shut out the sun.

It was hot, but shivery hot, as if the wood were feverish. The trees all looked the same as each other, with their smooth, acorn-coloured trunks. There was no sound at all, except for the hoofbeats of the horse, and the dull rustling of countless withered yellow flags of leaves. No birds sang.

"Why aren't there any birds singing?" asked the Prince in a nervous whisper.

"There aren't any birds," said the horse.

"Well, what is there then? It feels as if there's someone about."

And it did.

"Honnerdrin, probably," said the horse.

"Wh-what are h-honner— what you said?"

"Tree people."

"Are they— friendly?"

"No," said the horse.

"Couldn't we," said the Prince, "go some other way to get to the place we're going to – wherever it is?"

Just then the visor of the Prince's golden helmet came down over his face with a bang. The Prince panicked and shouted, until he realised he could still see out of the eye-holes in it. What he saw was that he and the horse had emerged into a clearing. At the far end stood a tall pavilion of scarlet velvet with some frightful-looking monsters embroidered on it in black. Next to the pavilion a gold bell hung from a solitary tree.

"I bet that bell says, 'I'm here, sound this and I'll come out and kill you', or something," said the Prince irritably. "Well, I'm not going to be caught a second time."

But he was, though in a most unexpected way. A thin brown hand came sneaking around the trunk of the tree, snatched the bell-rope and tugged it. The bell clanged noisily.

"Did you *see* that?" gasped the Prince. "That's not fair—" but there was no time for more.

Out of the pavilion came striding a terrifying figure in coal-black armour, scarlet plumes, and wielding an enormous axe.

"Who dares challenge me, the Champion of the Wood?" it roared. "Dismount and fight!"

"I didn't challenge you— It was—" began the Prince.

The figure roared at the horse. The horse reared. The Prince fell off.

The Prince picked himself up. He was certain the horse hadn't needed to rear at all; it couldn't have been that scared.

"Look," said the Prince reasonably, "I really didn't touch that bell. This hand came out of nowhere—" he broke off to avoid a ferocious axe blow.

The Prince drew the sword Vultikan had given him.

"Well, he said it would cut through anything," said the Prince doubtfully, and aimed. Both he and the Champion were very surprised as the sword sheared off the axe-head. Of the two, however, the Prince went on being surprised the longer, which allowed the Champion to hit him rather hard with the haft, and then jump on him as he fell over. The Champion's armour was very heavy and the Prince could hardly breathe, let alone move, but he cut about weakly with the sword, and presently the Champion said quite pleasantly, "I say, you can leave off now. You've wounded me badly and I surrender, only I can't get off you because of my armour."

The Prince wriggled and struggled and finally crawled out from under the Champion, and rolled him over on his back. The Champion pushed up his visor with one feeble hand, and smiled at the Prince in a 'don't worry about me, only a scratch, I'll be all right in a minute' kind of way.

"You needn't think I'm sorry for you," said the Prince angrily, "you started it."

"I didn't realise who you were," said the Champion.

"Who am I?" yelled the Prince, in a mixture of hope and foreboding.

"The Looked-for Deliverer, Slayer of the Dragon of Brass, Bearer of the Sword of Vultikan."

"Oh," said the Prince. He wiped his sword on the grass, and began to feel rather concerned after all.

"Do you want a doctor?" he enquired after a moment, and then wondered where on earth he would find one if the Champion said he did.

"No, no. I heal up very quickly – it's a spell my sister put on me when I decided I wanted to be a Champion and fight people. She likes magic and that kind of thing. Just give me a second, and I'll be as fit as a fiddle. Oh dear," he added apprehensively.

The Prince couldn't believe his eyes. Out of the trees came a violin, hopping along, coughing and sneezing and moaning that it felt sick. It crossed the clearing, and vanished among the trees on the other side.

"You have to be careful around here," said the Champion in a low voice, "not to say things like fit as a— well, like what I just said. They always try to show you up."

"Who do?"

"The Honnerdrin. They can take any shape they want, you see, and they listen to everything. When I decided to be a Champion, I thought this wood looked ideal, but if I'd known *they* were about, wild horses wouldn't have dragged me here— Oh!" he cried in despair.

Six neighing black stallions burst into the clearing, picked up the Champion, dragged him round his pavilion twice, dumped him back at the Prince's feet with a crash, and made off among the oaks.

"You see how it is," groaned the Champion.

The Prince helped him up and into the pavilion. The Champion sat on a scarlet chair and took off his helm. He had rather a nice, kind sort of face and black hair.

"If it's as bad as it seems to be here," said the Prince, "why don't you go somewhere else? And what do you want to fight people for, anyway?"

"Well, you have to choose very early on," said the Champion sadly, "and I thought it was a good idea then. But really, you know, I'd rather talk to people than fight them. They won't talk *after* a fight – they get huffy, or else they run away."

"Why don't you stop being a Champion?"

The Champion brightened.

"Do you know, I'd never thought of that? Why not, indeed? I won't be a Champion another minute."

All his armour immediately fell off on to the ground. Under it was a scarlet tunic with golden beetles embroidered on it.

The prince looked at the tunic and said, "You didn't tell me your name, by the way."

"Oh, didn't I? It's Gemant the Red."

"Your sister," said the Prince, "is she, by any chance, *Gemael* the Red, the Lady of the Waste? She whirls about a lot."

"That's it. Have you met her, then?"

"Several times," said the Prince.

"Yes. Nice girl," said Gemant. "Of course, I haven't seen her for ages, with her living in the Waste and me here in the woods, and all those mountains in between. She doesn't like whirling across mountains. How is she?"

"She seemed all right when I saw her last."

There was a clang from the bell outside. Gemant jumped to his feet in horror.

"There's a challenge, and I'm not a Champion any more! What shall I do?"

The Prince looked round the entrance flap and saw a Knight in purple armour in the clearing. He was riding what looked as if it might have started out to be a horse and then had changed its mind. It was bright mauve in colour with frightening yellow eyes, which it rolled around, and awful pointed teeth, which it snarled. Instead of a mane and tail, a hard spiky crest stood up on its head, and hard spiky things rattled behind it. Draped across it, in front of the Knight, was the form of a fair-haired maiden, presumably in a maidenly swoon.

"Are you the Champion of the Wood? If you are, come out and fight," cried the Knight in a menacing voice, having caught sight of the tip of the Prince's nose.

"Er, no," said the Prince, making the best of things, "I'm afraid he's not here at the moment – gone to visit a sick aunt."

"When will he be back? I'll fight him then."

"Let me see," said the Prince. "I should try again in five days' time. He's bound to be here by then."

The Knight gave a sound that might have been a growl of thanks, or a growl of anger, or simply just a growl. He wheeled the horse-thing, and they gal-loped off, sparks flying up all around them.

"You should be able to get away in five days," said the Prince to Gemant.

The horse put its head into the pavilion.

"Did you happen to notice," it asked, "that it was Ysome the Saffron he had in front of him?"

"Look," said the Prince, "really, I shouldn't bother if I were you. She's an enchantress – a bad one. She had me hunted all through the Castle of Bone – it's her Dragon of Brass I had to fight! *And* she was your sister's sworn enemy, Gemael told me so—"

"No, no," said Gemant firmly (he already had his armour on again and was running about packing things into a bundle), "I can't refuse to aid a lady in distress. I just couldn't face myself."

A Honnerdrin promptly walked into the pavilion, looking exactly like Gemant the Red, went up to him, stared him in the face, and walked out again. Gemant was too busy to notice.

"I'll have to get a horse somewhere," he worried, "and a sword now my axe has gone."

"You can have my sword," said the Prince. "*I'm* not going after her. You didn't *see* that purple knight."

"No, I couldn't take your sword. If Vultikan the Hoiler made it for you, I wouldn't be able to use it. Now, let me see, Gemael told me a spell for getting a horse . . ."

He wandered outside and began to say odd-sounding things with no result.

The Prince sat down and ate some fruit that was on the table in a golden bowl. But he had a feeling he was being watched, even though he couldn't see anyone, which must have been Honnerdrin.

After a time he got rather angry, and had an angry idea. He was tired of things happening to him, and he never seeming to make a decision of his own. So he got up, went out, looked at the oak trees, and said in a loud voice, "I know you're there, you Honnerdrin, and I suppose you know who I am – the Looked-for Deliverer, Slayer of the Dragon of Brass, Bearer of the Sword of Vultikan. Everyone else seems to think that's important, so I don't see why you shouldn't as well." The trees rustled noisily. "As you can change into any shape at all, I suggest," the prince went on, "that one of you change into a horse and another of you into a sword so Gemant can rescue Ysome. You can't mind that. She's just as much a troublemaker as you all are."

There was a long silence. The Prince noticed the horse staring at him in surprise, while Gemant looked positively terrified. The Prince had begun to wonder if he had done the right thing, when out of the trees came a black charger with red trappings, and a bright sword hopping along behind it.

"It, er, may be a trick," Gemant whispered to the Prince.

"No," said the Prince, feeling sure of himself all at once. "My name seems to be a powerful one, for some reason. Perhaps because of this Nulgrave thing they think I'm going to deliver them from."

'Ssh!" hissed Gemant, paling. All the trees seemed to shudder.

The Prince felt rather pale, too, suddenly.

"If you're all so scared of it, what *is* it?" he asked.

"No one knows," said Gemant, "but it's absolutely *awful*."

CHAPTER SEVEN

The Oak Wood

Gemant the Red and the Prince rode through the shadowy oak wood until it grew dark with evening.

"Are you sure we're going the right way?" asked the Prince, who wasn't sure of anything himself, especially as to why he had gone to look for Ysome after all.

"Oh, yes. You can see the hoof pocks and the scorch marks the Drumbil made quite clearly."

The Drumbil was, apparently, the awful mauve horse-thing the Knight had been riding.

The Prince wanted to stop and rest for the night, but Gemant said they ought to press on a bit farther, so they did. Blue starlight trickled down the trunks of the trees, and later the three moons appeared, one by one, and hung like peculiar white lanterns in the upper branches.

Soon after this, or so it seemed, the Prince woke up with a start, and realised he had fallen asleep on the back of the horse, and that it was now dawn. He looked round at Gemant, but *he* was very wide awake, and was urging the Honnerdrin horse to gallop, which it wouldn't.

"Look ahead!" he cried excitedly.

The Prince rubbed his eyes and did so. The oak trees came to an abrupt end at the edge of a broad river. On the far bank, a hilly heath toiled in grey-green folds towards the distant sunrise, and on the rizon stood up a curious, crooked black shape. The nce realised several things at once. First, that Gemant seemed to think the shape was where the purple knight was; secondly, that Gemant was trying to ride straight into the river, which looked dark and dangerous; and thirdly, that the sun seemed as if it might be rising on the wrong side of the sky.

He grabbed Gemant's bridle, seeing this as the most important thing at the moment, and said, "You can't, it's too wide to jump. You'll be drowned."

Gemant stopped bouncing about, and looked crest-fallen.

"However shall we cross?" he asked.

"Easy," said the Prince. To the wood he called out, "Remember me? One large boat, please, and an oar."

After a moment a boat appeared, and flopped into the water with a splash that wetted the Prince and Gemant from head to foot. The oar was next and managed to fall on the Prince's toe as he was dismounting.

"They don't like obeying anyone," said Gemant anxiously.

But he and the horses got into the boat, and the Prince rowed them all across, which took a long time. When they had struggled out of the water-reeds on the other side, and climbed a little rise up on to the heath, the Prince suggested they have breakfast. Gemant was unwilling to waste time, but the Prince insisted.

When they had finished, it was quite warm and sunny. Gemant lay down, and said, "Just rest for a moment," and fell asleep.

The Prince, delighted at any delay, followed his example.

The Prince had been dreaming about splashes and thuds, and it was a particularly loud thud that woke him. He sat up with a start, but everything was silent and very dark. It seemed odd, because he had been sure it was quite light when he fell asleep, but then it was probably only the wood, shutting out the sunlight.

Then he remembered that they had left the wood at the river bank.

"Gemant!" cried the Prince, in a loud, trying-to-be-quiet voice. Gemant took no notice. The Prince unkindly shook him, and Gemant woke up with a yell.

"Ssh!" warned the Prince. "Look!"

Gemant stared around them, and saw that they were surrounded by trees again, and by hot, shivery shadows.

"Well, there's the river behind us," he said, "and this is the heath. And you can just make out the knight's hold, still."

"I am holding still," grumbled the Prince.

Gemant looked confused, and decided to pretend the Prince hadn't said anything.

"The wood doesn't stretch very far up the heath, you see," he explained. "The trees end just in front of the next rise."

There was a colossal splash behind them. They both turned back and gawped at the river. Two or three oak trees seemed to be growing in it that hadn't been there before. Gemant and the Prince shrugged.

The Prince found his horse, but the Honnerdrin horse had vanished. So had the Honnerdrin sword. The Prince didn't ask for replacements.

As they were walking over the heath towards full daylight, several thuds happened behind them. Whenever they looked round, everything was still. After a time they stopped looking round.

"Do you know any songs?" the Prince asked Gemant very cheerfully.

"Oh, lots," said Gemant, very cheerfully.

There was a silence and three or four thuds.

"Sing something," said the Prince, very cheerfully.

Very cheerfully, Gemant began to sing.

"I met a maiden, fair and good,
With long yellow hair, in the acorn wood,
But when I asked with her to walk
She changed me into an apple stalk."

"That isn't the sort of song I meant," said the Prince.

There was another thud.

"Anyway," said the Prince loudly, "she couldn't have been fair and good if she turned him into an apple stalk."

"Perhaps she thought he might enjoy it," said Gemant lamely.

"You know," said the Prince, "I think it would be fun to have a race – to the end of the wood. Ready, steady, go!"

He and Gemant broke into a lurching run in their armour, and the horse shot ahead. It wasn't far, and soon everyone was out of the tree shadow into the noon sunlight.

"I won," said the horse.

"It doesn't matter who won," said the Prince, "we got out of that wood. Do trees always hop about like that?"

"Honnerdrin trees do," said the horse.

"Well, we're safe now," said the Prince, turning his back on the last tree.

They strode over the rise, and down the other side.

There were three loud thuds, one after the other.

"What?" said the Prince.

He and Gemant hurried on after the horse.

Thud! Thud! Thud! Thud!

"Don't look back, you'll only encourage them!" said the Prince. But Gemant did look back, and there were now five large oaks standing at the top of the rise, which had previously been treeless.

"It's no use, Horse," said the Prince. He scrambled into the saddle and helped Gemant scramble up behind him. "I know we're heavy, but do your best."

The horse broke into a slow walk.

"Faster! Faster!"

The horse trotted, sighed, and began to gallop.

Thud! Thud-thud! came behind them.

Gemant looked back and howled. The wood was no longer pretending not to move, for it too had burst into a gallop, and with its trees bounding over the ground in huge hops and leaps, leaves flying in the wind, branches snapping furiously, it was in close pursuit.

"What are we going to do?" despaired the Prince.

"When we get over the next rise," said the horse, "there'll be a ditch. Roll off into it and hide."

"How do you know there'll be a ditch?"

"How do you know there won't be?" asked the horse. "I shall ride on, and the wood will chase me, not having noticed the two of you are gone."

"Of course it'll notice. And besides, I need your help, and you may not come back."

Just then they rattled over the rise, the horse gave a peculiar wriggling rear, and Gemant and the Prince fell off into a ditch. As they lay there among the dead leaves and the mud, the oak wood went thundering by, each tree jumping over the ditch without pause. It was quite terrifying, however. Any minute it seemed one might misjudge the distance and land on top of them in the ditch instead. Finally it was over, and the cracking and thudding died away. They looked over the edge of the ditch, and saw the last trees thumping across the heath away to the right, which still left them a clear road to the hold of the Purple Knight (unfortunately, thought the Prince).

They crawled out and pulled the leaves from their hair. While they were doing this, the Prince suddenly noticed one solitary sapling standing quite still, behind them, on the other side of the ditch. He drew his sword.

"Stay where you are!" he yelled.

The sapling obeyed. But someone didn't. Around the side of the sapling, seeming to appear out of its trunk, came a thin, brown child with long, acorn-coloured hair and greenish-yellow eyes. It regarded the Prince with an amused sneer.

"This is my tree," it said, "and it didn't follow you. It's always been here by the ditch."

"Oh," said the Prince.

"B–be careful," whispered Gemant nervously. "It's a Honnerdrin child. They never appear in their true form unless they mean really bad mischief."

The Honnerdrin child looked at Gemant thoughtfully, and Gemant paled. Then it looked at the Prince and said, "Nulgrave is coming. You'd better be quick and stop it."

"What do you know about Nulgrave?"

But the child had disappeared, and there was only the oak sapling standing by the ditch.

CHAPTER EIGHT

The Tower of the Purple Knight

The Prince hadn't at any time liked the look of the Knight's hold, and now that he was close enough to see it properly, he still didn't like the look of it.

It was a tall tower made of some black metallic stuff, and out of its sides grew lots of other small towers, all craning and leaning and twisting in every direction. At the back of it the heath fell down into a dismal-looking chalk quarry. Round the foot of the tower was a circular black moat, and on the near side of this was a black stone with a black bell hanging from it.

"I suppose you have to sound that when you want to be let in," said Gemant.

"Well, I don't trust bells," said the Prince.

They stood about by the bell for ten minutes or so, and then Gemant said, "I say, I really think we ought to try. I mean we are supposed to be rescuing Ysome."

"Go ahead," said the Prince, edging back several places.

Gemant strode up to the bell and struck it. There was no sound at all, but an opening appeared suddenly in the tower, and out slid a drawbridge over the moat. Gemant marched straight on to it.

"Come back, you idiot!" yelled the Prince. But Gemant didn't, and so the Prince reluctantly followed him. They walked off the drawbridge into a totally black space, and in another second the drawbridge was drawn up behind them, and there was no light at all.

"Where are we?" cried Gemant, and his voice echoed back nastily four or five times.

"Where are *you*?" cried the Prince.

Next minute they collided with an armoury clatter, and nearly went deaf from armoury clattery echoes.

"I knew this was a mistake," muttered the Prince.

Just then an awful booming voice called out, "Who dares the hold of the Purple Knight?"

"If we keep quiet," whispered the Prince, "they might think there's no one here after all."

But Gemant wouldn't.

"I am the Champion of the Wood!" cried he, "and I have come to rescue the Lady Ysome."

The voice laughed horribly, and this time an opening appeared in one part of the darkness, filled with a bright purple glare.

"Enter, fool!" invited the voice.

"I wouldn't," said the Prince, "really – especially when he's being so rude."

But Gemant charged forward. The Prince ran after him, trying to pull him back, and the next minute they were through into a huge purple hall full of purple pillars, and purple light and purpleness.

The opening shut behind them with a bang.

"Trapped," remarked the Prince, without surprise. He sat down on a purple chair, feeling on the whole too fed up to be frightened. "I don't see why you had to rush in here, Gemant."

Gemant looked worried.

"I couldn't seem to help it," he said. "I didn't want to. And I didn't want to call out who I was either."

The Prince remembered how he had pulled the Brass Dragon bell in the Castle of Bone, and felt more sympathetic.

Just then two purple doors rolled open at the far end of the hall. Gemant and the Prince clutched each other, waiting for Something – probably a monster – to come slithering or crashing or leaping through, slavering at the jaws and with its blazing eyes glazed with hatred and blood-lust. It didn't. Nothing came through, in fact, except a stream of normal-looking light.

"Now don't—" began the Prince – but it was already too late.

And, as he ran after Gemant, it occurred to him that he didn't seem to have any choice either.

Beyond the door was—

"Aaaah!!!" cried the Prince.

"Whaaah!!!!!" cried Gemant.

A great white wind rushed up from their feet, their hair blew up from their heads, and the walls raced past at a terrific rate. They would have liked to say to each other, "Help! What is it? Help!" but the speed made them speechless. And then suddenly it was very dark, there was an awful splash and a lot of water in their eyes and ears, followed by a nasty, wet, dripping silence.

"What happened?" the Prince asked the darkness eventually.

"I think we fell down something," said Gemant. "Into something."

"Water. Only I can't understand why we're floating on top of it and not sinking because of our armour. And it's as black as when we first got into the tower."

"Not quite," said Gemant.

And after a time the Prince found he could just make out a dark rippling pool in which they were, with dim walls all round, and a very big circular black hole about five yards away.

"I wonder if that's a way out," said Gemant.

"Or a way in," said the Prince, and wished he hadn't.

"A way in – for what?"

And they both thought about the slavering monster with blood-lust glazed eyes they had been expecting upstairs, and wondered if it would come through the hole instead.

"You know," said the Prince, "I'm sure there's some way we could get out of this if we really thought about it." He was trying to ignore the fact that a faint light seemed to be coming out of the hole which hadn't been coming out of it a moment ago. "If only I could reach that brickwork higher up – it looks as if it might give a handhold. I wonder what would happen if I crawled up on top of you––?"

"I'd be pushed underwater and drown," said Gemant sadly.

The light was quite unmistakable now. It poured out from the hole and made silvery lacework on the water.

The Prince splashed hurriedly over to the far side of the pool.

"Look out!" he warned.

The next second something came out of the hole.

The Prince tried to get up the wall and failed. After a while he stopped trying and began to wonder why he hadn't been eaten. This was when he saw *what* had come out of the hole. It was three beautiful girls covered entirely, except for their faces, by long lustrous dark fur. Out of the fur at their temples grew two fine curling horns which reminded the Prince of someone or other, but in addition there were delicate gills fluttering just under their chins, and they seemed to have furry fish tails below the water. The silvery light came from a small globe the nearest one had on a thin chain around her neck.

"Who are you?" asked the Prince.

"We're a monster," said this girl, and they all tittered.

"Are you?" asked the Prince doubtfully, prepared by now for almost anything.

"Well, *he* thinks we are," said the girl scornfully.

"Do you mean the Purple Knight?"

"Yes. When we saw something moving about in the pool he thought it must be a monster, and so he built this tower all around the water, and he lures people, and has them thrown in here all the time. They don't drown because we put a magic on the water to keep them up, and then we come and show them out the back way. But *he* thinks the monster's eaten them." And they all giggled again. "Actually," added the girl, "we're Water Theels."

The Prince then remembered the white-haired Theel in the Castle of Bone, who had also been kind, if a little odd, and he wondered why such nice creatures always seemed to live in bad places with wicked things going on all around them.

"That's easy," said the girl, seeming to read his thoughts as the other Theel had done. "The bad places are where we can do the most good. Now come with us, in case *he* turns up to see if there are any bones floating about or anything. You'll have to hold your breath for the first part because that's under water, but it isn't very far."

It was rather farther than the Water Theels thought, being used to underwater, and it was very cold. But eventually the Prince and Gemant arrived in a dry warm cave, hung with pretty water-weed curtains, and with flowers growing out between the stones. A few globes like the one the girl carried, only larger, floated about in the roof, giving a soft clear light. The Water Theels sat with their furry fish tails still in the pool, and said a spell all together to make the Prince and Gemant dry again.

"All you have to do now is go through that opening there and down the passage, and you'll come out to the quarry behind the tower. There's a magic over the door so you won't be able to see the entrance once you're outside."

"This is very kind of you," said Gemant. "But can you tell us if a maiden was thrown into the pool yesterday or today – we came to rescue her, you see."

The Water Theels looked at each other.

"Do you mean a girl with fair hair and a yellow dress?"

"*That*'s her," said the Prince with distaste.

"We don't really think she needs rescuing," said the Water Theels, "she seems to be enjoying herself here."

"In that case," said the Prince, "I feel like rescuing her just to annoy her." He explained about the Castle of Bone.

"We can show you a way into the Knight's tower he doesn't know about," said the first Theel, "if that would help."

The Prince didn't really know why he wanted to get

mixed up in more trouble, he thought he'd had enough, but suddenly he realised he had to go back into the tower. 'It's all this Looked-for Deliverer business again I suppose,' he thought mournfully, as the Water Theels said a spell at the wall and showed him a flight of stairs once the stone had disappeared.

As they climbed the stairway the cave wall appeared again behind them so they could no longer see the Theels. They climbed and climbed and grew very tired.

"I wish that horse hadn't run off," said the Prince, "it nearly always seemed to know what to do."

Finally they came to a blank wall.

"Now what?"

"Look," said Gemant, and the Prince saw that there were several small round holes cut in the wall. Peering through one he found he was staring down at the purple hall he and Gemant had seen earlier, although now they seemed to be very high up near the ceiling. The hall was rather different too, because it was lit by hundreds of gold and rose-coloured lamps which made the purpleness rather attractive, and there was a huge table draped with cloth-of-gold and laid with gold dishes and whole-amethyst cups. Just then a fanfare sounded, and the awful booming voice they had been terrified by before called out rather soppily, "Honour and joy to His Glorious Worship the Purple Knight!"

Through some doors – not the ones through which Gemant and the Prince had fallen into the monster pool – came pipers blowing pipes, drummers beating drums, girls strewing ribbons, and, last of all ("Well, look at *that*!" cried Gemant) the Purple Knight, this time in purple velvet and a lot of gold embroidery, with Ysome the Saffron walking beside him, holding his arm. She had pearls and amethysts in her hair, and a new dress of primrose yellow velvet, and she was smirking.

"When I think," cried Gemant, "how much we endured to save her!" And he smote the wall a blow with his gauntleted fist. Which must, unfortunately, have set working some hidden spring, for, an instant after, he and the Prince, instead of leaning on the wall, found themselves falling from a height down into the hall, and landing with a frightful crash on the table among all the golden dishes.

Ysome and the ribbon-strewing girls screamed.

"Guard!" bawled the Purple Knight, and several large shadowy figures strode forward through the doors. "Explain yourselves," said the Purple Knight furiously.

The Prince and Gemant rolled around on the table trying to get up, and sending cups and plates spinning in all directions.

"No need for them to explain," said Ysome in a cold, spiteful voice. "Do you remember I told you, my lord, of the man who razed my castle to the ground, and then abandoned me in the Waste – homeless, and without any of my dear friends left to help me? This – is he!"

"Which one?" asked the Knight.

The Prince managed to get off the table.

"She means me. However, I only followed her to rescue her from you – I thought you abducted her."

The Knight looked uneasy.

"Well, er—" he began.

"It was a mistake," said Ysome, "and anyway he's

my friend now and my protector. I'm going to teach him all my magic."

The Knight looked pleased.

"So," he remarked, "there's nothing left for you to do. Shall we throw them to the monster, my dear?"

Ysome beamed. But Gemant, skittering off the table with a clatter, cried, "That already happened to us, and there isn't a monster there at all so your evil plans aren't worth a fig!"

"Oh Gemant," groaned the Prince. Gemant was surprised.

"Did I say something wrong?"

"No monster?" croaked the Knight. He looked shattered and near to tears.

"There are worse things," Ysome hissed in his ear. "Boiling oil-baths, vats of venom, drumbil dinners . . ."

The Knight cheered up.

"Of course there are, my dove. How silly of me. Guard!"

The guards advanced into the lamplight and the Prince saw them properly for the first time. They were seven feet tall, covered in iron armour, and under their helmets poked long-snouted faces with cold, glittering eyes, and ghastly tusks growing where their teeth ought to have been.

"Oh," whispered Gemant sickly. "*Beezles*."

The Prince desperately tried to recollect what the horse had told him about Beezles – if anything. He seemed to think they were worse than Bezzles and not so bad as Buzzles – or was it that they were better than Bezzles and *worse* than Buzzles, or was it that—? He stopped wondering as the two nearest seized him by the arms and dragged him out of the hall and up some dark stairs and finally, with a horrible gurgling growl, flung him face down on top of Gemant, and shut a metal door on them with a clang.

After a time the Prince sat up and looked around him. It was obvious Gemant and he were in some sort of dungeon. There was one small narrow window set in the wall. The Prince went over to it and looked out and saw a muddy twilight setting over the chalk quarry. Black things were flapping in circles over the quarry – they looked like Oggrings, but might only have been bats. From the distance came a faint roar of thunder.

Several wild schemes went through the Prince's mind. Could he squeeze through the window? Hardly. Could he jump the Beezles at the door? No. Did Gemant know any of Gemael's spells either for turning one small enough to squeeze out of narrow windows or big enough to burst open dungeon doors and frighten off Beezles? Gemant didn't. The Prince remembered the Egg which the Theel had given him at the Castle of Bone. He took it out and shook it and hoped it would break and his own personal secret – whatever it was – would hatch out and save him. Nothing happened to the Egg, so he put it back.

"I wish that horse was here," he said.

Footsteps sounded on the stairs. A Beezle threw open the door, and there stood the Purple Knight in full armour again.

"I have decided on your punishment," he cried.

"What's that noise?" interrupted the Prince, changing the subject. The Knight broke off and listened, and the Prince was rather surprised to note that there really was an odd noise. In fact, it sounded like the thunder he had heard before, except that it went on and on, and seemed to be getting louder and louder.

"A storm," said the Purple Knight. "Have no fear. You won't be bothered by storms much longer. I intend—" he broke off again, this time because the floor was very gently trembling. He strode to the window and looked out and gave a cry of alarm. Then, ignoring the Prince and the punishment he had in store for him, he turned and hurried out. The door was shut again.

The Prince and Gemant crowded to the window and stared down.

"Is it— ?" asked the Prince.

"I think it *is*," said Gemant.

In the twilight it was hard to see for sure, but as the rumbling got nearer and nearer, they could make out what appeared to be a great dark cloud bouncing over the ground towards the tower, and at the head of the cloud, galloping very fast, mane and tail flying behind it, was a determined-looking white horse with white and gold trappings.

CHAPTER NINE

Grey Magic

"It's that horse!" yelled the Prince in panic, "and the Honnerdrin wood's still after it! Whatever has it come back here for? Haven't we got enough troubles?"

The horse was by now running round and round the tower, skirting the quarry, the wood in full chase behind. The dungeon floor shook under the Prince's feet in a most frightening way, and hundreds of cobwebs and spiders which had been up in the beams for five years or more were falling on to his head in a grey, grumbling rain.

And then, all at once, the awful thudding stopped. The oak trees seemed to be all round the tower, standing quite still, and somehow looking at a loss. The horse had disappeared.

"I expect it's changed into a lion again to fool them," said the Prince in disgusted admiration.

"Can it change at will, then?" asked Gemant with interest.

"Oh yes," and remembering an earlier conversation with the horse, the Prince added, "It said you all could here."

"*I* can't," said Gemant.

"You haven't tried," said the Prince.

"Oh, I have. Lots of times."

The Prince thought this seemed a silly sort of thing to be discussing at a moment like this. He peered through the evening darkness, trying to see a lion somewhere, but was interrupted by the door being opened once again. This time the four Beezles bowed very low and muttered, "Please—growl, follow us— growl."

Astonished, Gemant and the Prince obeyed, and were soon back in the purple hall. The instant they arrived they were greeted by an incredible din, which turned out to be the Purple Knight and Ysome the Saffron shouting furiously at each other.

"Why didn't you tell me he was a powerful magician!" the Knight was bawling.

"He's not and I did!" Ysome shrieked. "And you said you could fight anyone!"

Then they saw the Prince. The Knight promptly threw himself on his knees.

"Mercy, Invincible Sir!" he cried

Ysome ran straight up to the Prince, clasped and kissed his hand, and, staring into his eyes, squeaked, "My deliverer!"

"Well really," said Gemant. "If anyone's that, it's me."

"Be quiet!" snapped Ysome, giving him a poison- ous glare. Then, sweetly to the Prince, "He made me pretend I was on his side – but I knew you'd rescue me. Oh, do you think I could ever really have *meant* those dreadful things I said?" She uttered a tinkling laugh at the very idea.

There came a terrifying thudding from outside, louder than ever. The floor trembled, and gold plates the Prince and Gemant hadn't knocked off the table before now jumped off by themseves. The Knight fell on his face. Ysome paled, but grabbed the Prince all the harder.

"S–so clever of you," she gasped, "to make the Honnerdrin help you."

Then, of course, the Prince understood. The Purple Knight and Ysome didn't realise the oak trees were just as intent on having his blood as they were; they thought he'd brought them here on purpose to attack the tower.

"But they don't—" began Gemant, bewildered. Quickly the Prince kicked him. Gemant yelled, but luckily stopped telling the truth, though his eyes were full of reproach.

"I'm the Looked-for Deliverer, remember," said the Prince loftily to Ysome. "Naturally the Honnerdrin do whatever I desire. Now Gemant and I must go out and speak to them – persuade them not to get too violent. You'd better stay here with the knight – and don't look out of any windows or they might fly at you."

"We won't," promised the Knight.

"We'll go the quickest way," added the Prince. He hurried Gemant across the hall, through the doors – and in another moment they were falling once more into the 'monster' pool.

The two Water Theels who appeared this time didn't seem at all surprised to see them. They seemed to understand the Prince's idea perfectly, though he had to explain to Gemant.

"If we go out this way we can hide until the wood goes away – if we'd gone through the door the trees would have jumped on us in a moment."

In the Theel-cave they found the third Water Theel. She was hanging her fifth garland of flowers round the neck of a big lion.

"It's the horse!" cried the Prince. "How did you get in?"

"Through the cave entrance," said the horse-lion.

"But there's magic on the entrance so it can't be seen from the outside."

"That's right," said the horse-lion.

The Prince decided not to pursue this line of questioning.

"When will the wood go away?" he asked instead. He could still hear the thudding as all the trees angrily stamped on the spot, though it sounded much fainter here, and the floor didn't shake.

"Once the tower falls, probably," said the horse-lion. "They think it's ours, and we're all inside it."

"But how—" began the Prince.

A rattle of metal pieces falling off the sides of the tower and into the quarry interrupted them.

"You mean," said the Prince, "they'll shake the tower to pieces by thudding?"

"Yes. It's vibration."

"Who?"

"What about these ladies?" asked Gemant anxiously.

"Oh, we'll be quite all right," said the Water Theels. "The walls of our cave are very strong and we can soon clear our pool with magic."

From outside there came a tumbling crash, and a splash as something fell into the moat.

"There goes one of the towers,' said Gemant with conviction. "Or perhaps it was part of the roof."

Things fell thick and fast after that and it became quite frightening – at any rate, the Prince thought so. He was sure that at any moment the cave would col-

82

lapse all round them, but it stood firm. There were tremendous bangs and groans and concussions over-head, however, and eventually one really terrible ex-plosive thud followed by clattering and rolling sounds, screams, yells, and, finally, total silence.

"Isn't it quiet?" whispered the Prince nervously.

He realised then that the oak wood had stopped stamping.

They went to the cave entrance and looked up at the top of the quarry, and the wood had gone away.

"Once the tower fell, they felt they'd done enough," said the horse-lion.

"I should think so," said the Prince. He went out into the moonlit quarry – now full of broken towers, metal plates, window frames and an armchair – and stared up at the heap of black rubble above. "You know, this reminds me of the Castle of Bone . . ."

It then reminded him even more, for out of the heap came crawling the Purple Knight in badly dented armour, and Ysome, her dress in rags and the remains of an ancient crow's nest caught up in her hair. She saw the Prince at once, and pointed her finger down at him.

"You!" she screamed. "Again you destroy my home! I will be revenged – I swear it – by – by – by Nul-grave I swear it!" Having sworn, she looked rather scared, but she only had to glare at the Prince to become angry again. "By the four elements – Earth, Air, Fire, Water – I will work Grey Magic against you because of this."

The Purple Knight seized her arm.

"No, no – too dangerous—"

But she shook him off.

"Boiling-oil, vats of venom – you'll be pleased to be put into them by the time I've finished with you, sir Prince!"

The Prince, who was quite worried by now, tried to get back into the Theel-cave and, sure enough, couldn't find it because of the magic on the entrance. Suddenly a lion's paw appeared out of nowhere, hooked its claws into his arm, and hauled him through a blank wall which turned out to be the cave opening.

"Ow!" cried the Prince ungratefully. "Now look what you've done! She's going to put some awful curse on me, and she's going to work *Grey Magic* – whatever that is."

A silence fell in the cave, a silence both deep and full of mysterious meaning. Feeling left out, the Prince demanded, "What is it?"

The horse-lion said, "Ysome is the key to the coming of Nulgrave. Once she works Grey Magic, Nulgrave will be free to sweep into the world."

"What? I don't understand. How do you know?"

"It came," said the horse-lion, "into my head, and seemed the right thing to say at the time."

"Are you sure this will work?" worried the Prince, draping the wet water-weed around his neck and trying not to scowl as it dripped inside his armour. The Water Theels had put a magic on it so that for a time he – and Gemant and the horse-lion, who were also wearing water-weed – would be invisible to the vengeful inhabitants of the fallen tower.

"Oh, yes. But only for a little while, so do hurry," said the Theels.

The horse-lion licked their pretty faces and patted them gently with a paw. The Prince had never seen it show affection before.

Once outside the cave, they struggled up the sides of the quarry. At the top the heath had been dreadfully churned up by the Honnerdrin trees. There seemed to be no one about among the rubble of the tower except two of the mauve horse-things with spikes that were called drumbils. They snarled and rolled their eyes at the sky, but didn't seem to see the Prince and his companions, which was no doubt just as well.

Soon the three were hurrying over the hilly heath.

"Will it be dawn soon?" asked the Prince.

"No. Why?"

"I thought I could see some light back there."

"The sun never rises on that side of the sky," said the horse-lion.

"Well it rises just about on every other side, then. And there *is* a light. Turn round and you'll see."

They turned and looked back. A kind of grey glow was curling up the sky behind them.

"That's where the Knight's hold was, isn't it?" asked Gemant.

"Lie down on the ground," said the horse-lion.

"On the ground?" said the Prince. "It's damp – and also it's very hard to get up again in this armour—"

He got no further. The horse-lion nudged him over and he fell with a rattle on the grass. Gemant went over next, and the lion jumped on top of them. The Prince had a sudden horrible thought that it might have decided to eat him, but then he stopped worrying about that. A huge howling wind came gushing over the heath, a wind that would have blown them all flat in any case if they had been standing up. The grass bent right over, and racing, black, tattered clouds swallowed the stars and moons. Things came

blowing past – a few uprooted trees among them –
and fell around them as the wind spluttered and died
down as quickly as it had risen.

"What was it?" gasped the Prince. "Not – Nulgrave?"

"No," said the horse-lion.

"Then it was that Ysome and her Grey Magic I'll
bet."

He sat up and looked behind him, but the glow had
faded from the sky. There was an uneasy quiet.

"Let's get on then," said the Prince.

So, pretending to forget the grey glow and the wind
and Nulgrave and all the rest of it, they got up and got
on.

CHAPTER TEN

The Marsh

The Prince woke in time to see the real dawn. He was lying near the ashes of the fire Gemant had made the night before in a small valley, surrounded by gorse-jacketed hills. It was too chilly to sleep, but not for Gemant. The horse-lion wasn't there, but it tended to go off by itself in the morning, the Prince had noticed. The Prince lay on his back and watched the sugar-pink sky and the lavender clouds wallowing in it like furry, disgruntled whales in a pink sea. There was a mist over the heath that made it difficult to tell where the sky ended and earth began, and suddenly a bright thing came glittering across the mist.

The Prince jumped to his feet. It was a silver chariot shaped like an open flower, being pulled over the sky by three silver horses with fiery wings. He remembered how he had seen one on his first night in this strange world, but he couldn't work out why he was so excited at seeing one again – unless it was because it looked so romantic and beautiful. And then the chariot dipped gracefully.

"They're going to land on the heath!" cried the Prince aloud.

Next second the horses had leapt forwards across the gold spokes of the rising sun and they and the chariot vanished in the mist.

The Prince scrambled up the side of the hill, stumbled over the gorse, aiming for the place where he thought they had come down. The mist was golden now and he couldn't see where he was going. He banged into a dead tree, and apologised, put his foot into a hole full of water, and finally got tangled in a bush. While he was getting out of this he saw a cool gleaming ahead of him, and heard a soft strange tinkling that would have scared him if it hadn't sounded so gentle.

The Prince swallowed and went towards the gleam.

The chariot had settled on the grass, the three horses rustling their flame-feathered wings slowly, and nodding their silver heads so that little drops of crystal on their bridles sparkled and tinkled. In the chariot stood a handsome man and a beautiful girl in curious rainbow clothes. They were very pale – almost transparent; his hair was a deep rich gold like the sun's rays, and hers a delicate lavender, the colour of the clouds.

The Prince's knees trembled and his mouth felt dry though he wasn't certain why because he wasn't afraid. He wanted to say something to the people in the chariot – the Sky People, the horse had called them – but he couldn't think of what to say.

And then the man shook the crystal-beaded reins, the horses lifted their flame-flower wings, and the chariot rose upwards, over the Prince's head, and was gone.

The Prince stared around him.

"But I didn't have time to ask—" he said. "I mean I wanted to say that—"

"What?" asked a big lion shouldering through the mist.

"It was them – the Sky People—" said the Prince.

"Oh," said the horse-lion, "they never talk."

"Where are you?" an anxious voice howled behind them. Gemant had woken up.

As they trudged on over the heath the Prince became irritable. The mist had lifted, but the air was damp and cold, and there seemed to be a funny sort of disturbance in it from time to time.

"Are you supposed to be going somewhere, Gemant?" he demanded abruptly.

"No," said Gemant. "I just thought I'd follow you."

The Prince stopped.

"We might just as well stay here then," said the Prince. "Or go back the way we came."

But as soon as he stopped he had that feeling again that he had to go on. So after a minute or so of grumbling he did.

"When Gemael and I were very small," Gemant said suddenly, "we were very close."

"What's that got to do with anything?"

"Well," said Gemant eagerly, "we always seemed to know when the other one was in trouble. I remember once I was playing with my pet Skook—"

"Your pet what?"

"Skook. And I—"

"What's a Skook?"

"Oh," Gemant seemed rather surprised the Prince didn't know. "It's a sort of round fluffy thing. All children have them; they play with you and teach you the alphabet and the eleventy times table – things like that. Well, as we were playing, I suddenly got a cold feeling just here—" he tapped the end of his nose, "and I thought: Gemael needs me!"

"Did she?" asked the Prince.

"Yes. She'd fallen into a pond. I rescued her," he added proudly.

The Prince thought Gemant seemed to have a thing about rescuing people. The annoying muzzy effect in the air started again just in front of him. The Prince rubbed his eyes. It seemed to be getting worse.

"And then there was the time," said Gemant, "that Gemael suddenly cried—I say, what's that?"

"What had she seen?" asked the Prince.

"No, I meant, *I* said 'what's that?'"

"What?"

"There," said Gemant.

They all stopped and looked at the muzziness.

"You know, it reminds me of the whirling that always happened just before Gemael appeared," said the Prince.

They stared at it expectantly, but after a moment or so it faded away.

"My nose feels cold," said Gemant worriedly. "It has all morning. I think Gemael's in danger and she's trying to appear here instead of wherever the danger is, and something's stopping her. What shall I do?"

"Think about something else?" suggested the Prince.

"But I'm worried—"

"Ssh!" interrupted the horse-lion.

They had just come over a little rise, and in front of them the land levelled out and became a dull wet green marsh with large areas of water glinting in the distance. Two perfectly ordinary-looking men in green jerkins were walking in the mud and reeds.

"Will they attack us?" asked the Prince promptly in a low voice.

"Probably not, unless you say something to upset them," said the horse-lion.

"Then why did you say 'Sssh!'?"

"You can never tell," said the horse-lion.

The two men had by now looked up and seen them. Instead of attacking they started to run away as fast as they could.

The Prince and Gemant walked over the rise, but the horse-lion became a horse first because it said it didn't like getting its paws wet. When they reached the nearest reed-bed ten green ducks flew up quacking, and fled away.

"Well, really," said the Prince. "We're not *that* frightening."

He could feel his feet sinking in the marsh and became nervous. He walked along staring at the ground and testing the mud before he stood on it, and so he wasn't aware of the *thing* until he banged right into it.

"I'm so sorry—Ah!" he yelled.

He had collided with a black wood pole, very slimy, and on top of it was a shiny green skull with long green hair.

After a minute or so he realised it wasn't real but a skull carved from a green stone, and the 'hair' was actually some lichen which was growing on it.

"Oh—ha!" he laughed hoarsely. He looked round and saw Gemant and the horse had taken another path and were some distance away. "Hey! Come and look at this!" he cried.

Just then the green skull jaws parted and the skull said conversationally, "Whither goest thou?"

"What!" screamed the Prince.

"Whither goest thou?" obligingly repeated the

skull.

The Prince backed away, slid on some mud and fell over.

"Dost seek the Mad Witch?" asked the skull kindly.

"Help!" shrieked the prince.

"Her lair lies yonder," said the skull, and swung round to point to the right.

Gemant came charging through the reeds, trying to wield his axe, having forgotten he no longer had one. The horse came more slowly.

"It's only a witch-mast," said the horse.

"A w-witch what?"

"A witch generally puts one up near her lair so it can tell travellers how to find her."

The skull suddenly burst into maniacal laughter. "Oh, but she is a mad witch, by my troth!" it cackled.

The Prince got up angrily.

"Well, I don't want to know how to find her, thank you."

Gemant seized his arm.

"Perhaps she can help me rescue Gemael!"

"Perhaps she can't!"

"The Mad Witch doth know all. She will mayhap aid thee. Yonder lies her lair!"

Gemant hurried off the way the skull pointed at once. The horse leisurely followed Gemant.

Having no choice, the Prince stamped after them, feeling confused.

Soon there was a stretch of reed-fringed water, and in it lay a sort of island, very flat, with some odd-looking trees growing over it. There was another pole at the water's edge, but instead of a skull on it there was a round stone with strange signs carved into the surface.

"Well, that must be where her lair is, on that island," said the Prince. "And it's probably dangerous to swim out there – you never know what might be in the water!"

"I don't care," said Gemant stubbornly, "I've got to help Gemael."

And so saying he plunged in and promptly sank up to his waist.

"You can't swim in armour, anyway," said the Prince.

A weird noise came from the carved stone on the pole. Suddenly a narrow path appeared over the water, stretching from the shore to the island.

"It's a trick," said the Prince.

Gemant struggled up on to the path and began to hurry across.

"It must be like the tower again. He can't help himself."

The Prince got on to the path and followed, and the horse came daintily after him, shaking mud off its hooves. It took only a short while to reach the island.

The trees were twisted around each other and bowed together like a group of thin people with their arms linked, plotting something unpleasant. It was gloomy and green, and there were weeds which lashed out and stung them as they passed.

And then they had reached a kind of clearing, and at the other end of it was something that made even Gemant stop and wonder if he ought not to go away again rather fast.

CHAPTER ELEVEN

The Mad Witch

A gigantic spider's web hung among the trees, the top of it lost in the top branches, the bottom brushing the ground, the sides of it stretching for several feet. There was a cold glitter all over it for it seemed to be spun of thin steel, and it shifted and whispered abrasively in the breeze. At the very centre of the net hung—

"What is it?" gasped Gemant. "It can't *be* a spider . . . can it?"

"Yes," said the Prince spitefully, "it could be and it probably is."

"It's a large oval thing, big enough to be a small house," said the horse. "Perhaps the Witch lives in it."

There came a scream of insane laughter from the oval thing, and then a sort of door was flung open in it. And there stood the Mad Witch in the middle of her steel web.

"Well, she's certainly mad," muttered the Prince. "She lives in a spider's web and she's dressed like a wasp."

The Witch heard him. She gave a shriek of joy or fury and jumped straight down from the web into the clearing, landing upright and with perfect balance. Her thin body was clad in a tight furry wasp dress of black with yellow stripes around it, and out of the dress poked incredibly long skinny arms and feet and neck, and a face that was all one long nose and one mad grin and two malicious black eyes. A cascade of fierce grey hair poured from the Witch's head to her feet, covered by a green lace veil made from weeds and secured in various places by the pincers of small green crabs. The Prince didn't think they were real at first but he soon noticed how they wriggled about and realised they were.

The Witch darted straight up to the Prince, poked him in the chest with a long forefinger and squawked, "I am the Mad Witch! I know all the hidden secrets of the world! What knowledge do you wish to beg from me? Eh? Eh?"

The Prince backed away

"I don't want a thing," he said. "Ask *him*."

The Witch promptly flew at Gemant.

"My sister is in deadly peril!" cried Gemant. "Please help me to save her."

"Nonsense!" screamed the Witch.

"But she is – truly – I've always known when she needed me—"

"Half a measure of eel's spit would do!" shrieked the Witch.

"She *is* mad," said the Prince.

"Silence, slave!" the Witch howled. "Or I shall sting you! Now. Sisters, sisters. How many do you have?"

"Only one – Gemael – and she—"

"Rubbish! Save her? Why?"

"She's very dear to me."

"I don't give my services for nothing," snapped the Witch. "What will you give me if I agree to help you? Bah!!"

Gemant seemed to have become used to the Witch's way of talking.

"Anything," he said.

The Witch pondered, a crafty gleam in her eyes.

"Then give me," she cried triumphantly, "the rose growing out of your forehead."

Gemant looked around him wildly, clutching at his brow.

"What shall I say?"

"Say 'yes'," said the horse.

"Yes," said Gemant.

The Witch leaned forward, clasped the air in front of Gemant's eyes and tugged.

"Ow!" yelled Gemant in obvious pain.

"Got it!" screamed the Witch.

"I don't understand," said Gemant. "There wasn't any rose growing out of me, but it hurt when she pulled it off me – only she didn't."

"Now – nonsense!" cried the Witch, turning to the Prince. "What'll *you* give me? Eh?"

"I," said the Prince, "am not asking for anything, so I don't have to give *you* anything."

"You do, or I won't help your friend."

"What do you want?" asked the Prince incautiously.

"Your eyes!"

The Prince turned pale.

"Say," said the horse, "they don't work properly."

"They don't," said the Prince.

"Don't what?" demanded the Witch.

The Prince was trembling so much he could only say, "The horse told you—"

"Horses can't talk," shouted the witch.

"My eyes—don't work properly—" gasped the Prince.

"Ah!" The Witch seemed to accept this. "*Bah! Wait!*" She pointed at the Prince and made a circling motion with her finger.

"Wrinkle skinkle twitcheth snout,
    Sniff and snuff and find it out!"

The Prince had a sudden horrible sensation as if a million small ants were running all over him, and then the Witch grinned very hard and said, "In your pocket is an Egg. *That*'s what I want. Nonsense!"

The Prince looked at the horse.

"Now what shall I do? The Theel told me I mustn't let anyone else have it in case it hatched out and then they knew—" The Witch interrupted by leaping forward, grabbing the Egg out of his pocket and skipping back clutching it in her skinny hand.

The Prince ran after her and the witch spun round on one foot, pointed at him, and cried, "Zellezor-in-Parrapax!"

And the Prince found himself rooted to the spot, not able to move any part of himself except his eyes.

The Witch looked him over.

"Your eyes seem all right to me, young man. Two ounces of Rend-fangs at the double!! You!" She pointed at Gemant. "You will now toil for me for three days, after which I will work the spell to save your brother."

"Sister," nervously corrected Gemant.

"Blister," agreed the Witch.

"Couldn't you—do it first—only I think she may be in awful danger—"

"Very well," said the Witch surprisingly. "Where is she?"

Gemant explained as best he could between the witch's interruptions of "Brimstone!" and "Bah!"

The Witch gave a sudden great leap into the air, came down on her back on the ground, rolled her eyes and waved her arms, jumped up again, ran round in a circle three times and screamed several seemingly meaningless phrases.

"'Tis done," she concluded, sounding rather like the green skull. "Thy sister shall be restored to thee in four days – when you've finished toiling. Until then she's in a safe in-between place and won't be hurt. And just in time," she added. Leaping into the air again, she wailed, "Nulgrave is come. Woe unto the Land of Sinners whom God hath forsook!"

The Prince, unable to move, blinked his eyes rapidly in fear. Nulgrave had *come*!

But the Witch didn't seem to care any more.

In a series of impossible bounds up to and down from her oval house in her steel spider's web she collected several peculiar objects and laid them at Gemant's feet.

"I expect hard work," she said, "or I'll reverse the spell on your blister."

The first thing the Witch wanted Gemant to do was nothing whatever to do with the objects she had brought. It was to chop down all the trees around the clearing, presumably to make it bigger. Gemant set to work with a will swinging the Witch's large axe (which he found hidden in a puddle) as he had done with his own when he was Champion of the Wood. However, his armour was rather a nuisance. Eventually the horse suggested that he say, "I don't want to *be* a champion, or fight, or rescue anyone," whereupon the armour fell off on to the ground.

The Prince felt rather angry because no one took any notice of him. He had a nagging worry they might forget him and leave him here for ever.

The shadows lengthened, and by sunset Gemant had felled all the nearest trees. The Witch came leaping down and said he could rest for the night. Gemant, who hadn't even paused for lunch, curled up by the horse and fell asleep at once. The Witch came up to the Prince, spun round on her foot the other way and said, "Pellepor-in-Zarrazax!"

The Prince found he could move again. He stretched and groaned and the Witch thrust a large jar at him.

"Don't think – Nonsense! – you're getting out of *your* toil. Take the jar and sprinkle the seeds in it round the clearing ten times."

The Prince didn't argue. He went round the clearing as she had told him, throwing out handfuls of seeds as he went. It seemed to take a long time and the jar never emptied. After the tenth circle he was only too glad to roll limply in his cloak on the other side of the horse and go to sleep as Gemant had done.

They were both woken early by the Witch who was dancing round the clearing and singing a mad song. Scattered about were the fallen trunks of the trees Gemant had cut down the day before, but the clearing was now ringed with an even thicker fuller growth of trees.

"It must have been those seeds," said the Prince.

"Awake! Ah!" cried the Witch. "Up, and cut down all the trees."

The Prince, who was thirsty, asked her for a glass of water. The Mad Witch snapped her fingers and produced one from the air. She then threw the water in the Prince's face.

"Better? Now. Here's a second axe. Off with you."

At noon the Prince insisted that he and Gemant rest, so they shared the last of Gemant's provisions and sat for ten minutes under a tree before the Witch leaped down and ordered them back to work.

As dusk fell the Prince and Gemant leaned wearily on their axes, having cut down all the new trees.

They slept soundly but dawn brought the Witch with two jars under her arm.

"Third day," she screeched in their ears. "Sprinkle this round the clearing forty times, then deal with what comes up."

The Prince and Gemant, sighing, got up and did so. It took until noon. They were expecting a new crop of trees to cut down, but at first nothing happened. Then suddenly all the fallen trunks bounced upright, twisted round each other and somehow joined together, and changed, slowly but horribly, into an enormous, long, greenish prickly snake-creature with a very large mouth full of thorns instead of teeth and a pair of leaf-green eyes.

There was nowhere to run because the snake-creature was all round the clearing where trees had been – and this meant all round them. It wriggled its 'neck' about and stared at them, blinking solemnly, and then pushed itself nearer until its huge face was resting on the ground a few inches from the Prince's feet.

"Heaven help us!" whispered Gemant. "It could swallow us whole."

"Try being friendly," said the horse.

100

"What? *How?*" demanded the Prince in a shaky voice.

"Pat it," said the horse.

Very, very nervously, the Prince sidled up to the gigantic prickly face, and patted its head. A fearsome growling immediately issued from the thorny jaws. The Prince yelled.

"It's only purring," said the horse.

The Prince patted again, and the noise got louder. He scratched about among the bristles, and the green, rather lovely eyes gazed up at him adoringly. The Prince's heart warmed to it, and he suddenly felt quite silly with relieved affection.

"You're a nice old thing, aren't you," he laughed. "Who's a nice old thing, then? Who is, then, is it you? Yes, of course it is, purr, purr. Who's a dear old prickly snakey?"

Encouraged, Gemant joined in, and the purring grew so loud they could hardly hear what they were saying to it.

After a while the tree-snake put out a delicate green tongue and panted gently.

"Perhaps it's thirsty," said Gemant.

"Well, it's no good asking that witch for any water. I wonder if the marsh water would be all right?"

Apparently it would, because the tree-snake became excited and licked him and wriggled about. So they guided it through the remaining trees to the edge of the island, where, with a delighted roar, it buried its head and golluped up a few gallons of liquid.

They passed the rest of the afternoon very pleasantly, sitting on the island's edge talking to the tree-snake and putting their tired feet in the cool water.

About sunset they heard the Witch shrieking for them and went back.

"Ah! Nonsense! You've done it!" she screamed, obviously pleased. "I've always wanted one of those. Bah!" She embraced the tree-snake, which wagged its tail and knocked Gemant over. "Right. Third day of toil finished. You can go. Rubbish!"

Gemant staggered as all his armour reloaded itself on to him.

"But my sister – where is she?"

"A quart of Stoat's bane, and stir it well!"

Gemant looked upset.

"You did say—"

"Brimstone! She'll turn up. Be off now! Or I'll reverse the spell! Nonsense!"

Gemant turned sadly away, but the Prince ventured, "About my Egg—"

"Eggs – pegs!"

"It's rather important—"

The Witch folded her skinny arms over her furry wasp dress.

"Zellezor—" she intoned slowly, "—In—"

The Prince fled.

Looking back a safe number of trees away, he saw the Mad Witch and the tree-snake chasing each other happily round the clearing to the accompaniment of thunderous purrs.

"Well, I'm glad someone's satisfied," he moaned.

CHAPTER TWELVE

The Kreeler

A copper-red dusk lay over the green of the marshes as they floundered through the reeds. Before long they saw a village of strange round mud and stone houses built on a platform on stilts. A few men in green jerkins – just like those they had seen earlier – promptly ran out of sight, yelping in fear.

"Perhaps they think we're the Witch," said Gemant.

"We don't look a bit like the Witch," said the Prince thankfully.

He still hoped they might be able to stay the night at the village in the warm and dry, but a woman in a green kirtle appeared suddenly out of a house with a handful of sharp stones which she flung at the Prince.

"Be off!" she cried.

The stones clattered against his armour.

"We only wanted—"

"I know who you are – the Looked-for Deliverer – and I know there's a curse on you, and danger follows you like a hungry Skolk. We'll have none of that here. Take yourself away!"

And she threw a particularly nasty stone. The Prince ducked, and the stone hit Gemant's helm and knocked him over. The Prince, feeling guilty, went to help him up. When this was accomplished, the woman had vanished, obviously feeling she'd done all she could. And she had. They turned away into the red darkness and splashed through huge puddles the colour of bronze.

They spent a damp uncomfortable night by a smoking fire. The horse slept very well, but the Prince was too uneasy, and Gemant was too worried.

"If Nulgrave *has* come," said the Prince, "where is it?" He was hoping the Mad Witch had made a mistake. "And, if Ysome's out to be revenged on me – where is *she*?" He glanced round hastily, just in case. "Don't worry," he comforted Gemant, "Gemael will probably whirl in tomorrow. That witch may have been mad but her spells worked perfectly," he added with a shudder.

Towards morning they dozed.

The Prince woke about an hour after dawn to drizzle and a cold, salt-smelling wind. The horse was drinking from a pool nearby.

"I can smell salt," said the Prince.

"The marsh leads into the sea," said the horse.

"Which sea?"

"*The* sea. There's only one."

"Oh," said the Prince.

As they had no food, they didn't waste time on breakfast, and were soon moving on. Gemant looked very downcast.

"Do you know any more cheerful songs?" asked the Prince, hoping to make him feel better.

"Lots," said Gemant sadly.

After half an hour or so, the Prince suggested he sing one.

"I couldn't," said Gemant.

"That's that then," said the Prince, and himself

broke into a song he said was called "Heave-Ho!", or "The Drunken Sailor", or something – he wasn't sure. He wasn't sure of the words, either, but it made a good deal of noise, which was what he felt they all needed.

The ground began to go up and down again, though it was still very wet. And then suddenly there was nothing ahead but some chalky boulders, a few reed-beds, and a long, cold, grey stretch of something the Prince had thought was part of the sky.

"The sea?" he asked.

Large grey clouds herded overhead and a wind was blowing up, pushing the waves against each other. To the left was a range of low cliffs over which the sun showed in a small bright circle.

Gemant took out a scarlet handkerchief and blew his nose.

"She had grey eyes," he faltered.

The Prince, scared Gemant would break down altogether, looked hastily round for something to distract him.

"Look at that rock on top of the nearest cliff," he cried. "It's shaped just like a gigantic man with a gigantic fishing net."

"It is," said the horse.

"Well, I just said it was."

"It *is* a gigantic man. And as he would look altogether silly holding a fishing net of ordinary dimensions, he holds instead a net of the correct proportions, which is therefore similarly gigantic."

The Prince, who hadn't understood a word of this, turned round and found it wasn't the horse who had spoken. *His* horse was being a lion, and frisking in among the wavelets despite what it had said about not liking wet paws. The newcomer was also a horse, and also white, but it had gills and little fins as well, and instead of back legs a pearly fish tail. It had swum up in the pool behind him, and was now lying elegantly on a reed-bed.

"I might add," added the new horse, "that he is altogether a repulsive creature, and what he is doing is quite repulsive. He catches sea-maidens in his net, *and* sea-horses if he can, but, being less stupid than the sea-maidens, we generally extricate ourselves in time. He is known as the Kreeler."

Again the Prince felt he hadn't really understood properly. The horse – sea-horse? – seemed to have an odd way of talking. But it also looked rather impressive, so the Prince said, "Thank you."

"Do not mention it," said the sea-horse. "One is pleased to be helpful."

But Gemant was roused to action.

"Do you mean to say that monster up there *catches* mermaids in his net? What does he do with them?"

"One does not like to think," said the sea-horse. "Certainly, they are never seen again."

The change in Gemant was quite astounding.

"Oh for my axe!" he cried. "Or a sword! Nay! I'll tackle him with my bare hands."

"Don't be daft," said the Prince.

Gemant was already plunging up the marshy shore, shaking his fist.

"What a courageous young man," remarked the sea-horse. "He must be the Looked-for Deliverer."

"Thank you," said the Prince again, though rather angrily this time. He ran after Gemant shouting, "Come back!" and "Help, horse!"

The lion looked up from the waves, and trotted in a

leisurely way after him.

As they got nearer to the cliff, the Prince was able to see the giant more clearly, not that he wanted to. He had thought Vultikan the Hoiler was enormous, but he had only been about nine feet high. *This* creature was much bigger than that. It seemed to be dressed in black clothes, and black hair flittered round its head in the wind like a flight of Oggrings. The long net was stretched from cliff to sea, and dipped into it, for here the water seemed very deep.

Gemant ran to the rocks that formed the base of the cliff and began to climb them, intending to arrive at the top behind the Kreeler. He made a frightful din, but the Kreeler was probably too large to hear it.

Eventually Gemant reached his goal and lay panting on the cliff among some boulders. The Prince dragged himself up beside him.

"Now what do you think you can do?" he demanded. "Look at the size of him."

The lion joined them, and sat washing its paws.

"I'll think of something," said Gemant deperately.

The Kreeler gave a yell. The cliff shook from the noise.

"He's caught something," said the Prince in horrified interest. "Look, he's started to haul the net up."

Sickly, they watched the great arms hauling, and then the net, dripping water and seaweed, appeared over the cliff-top. A huge wicker basket lay a few feet away from their hiding place among the boulders. The Kreeler now turned with the net in one brawny hand, and leaned towards the basket. The Prince nearly screamed in terror as the gigantic dark evil face came looming over him, its little red eyes winking with pleasure. The giant flipped up the wicker basket lid, emptied the net into it, and pulled the lid down again. Then, with a chuckle, the Kreeler took up his former position on the cliff edge, lowered the net again, and sat waiting for a new catch.

Gemant was up in a moment, straining to lift the wicker basket lid. The Prince and the lion pushed at the other two sides. Unwillingly, the lid lifted a fraction. They gave a thrust, and the lid flew up, poised for a moment deciding which way to fall, then flopped on to its back with a crash. The Prince waited in fear for the Kreeler to turn round but he didn't. The Prince thought he must be deaf as well as evil.

They scrambled up the wicker sides and peered into the depths of the basket, and there in the darkness was a green and blue struggling mass, weeping and shrieking to itself.

"Be quiet!" yelled the Prince into it, no longer bothering about the deaf giant. "We've come to help you."

The noise died away a little, and pale arms and fins waved at them and voices cried piteously, "Save us!"

They arranged that the lion should dig its claws into the wicker to anchor itself, and hold Gemant by his scarlet sash as he leaned down into the basket. He would then grab the mermaids one by one and the Prince and the lion would haul them all up. This they did. On the whole the mermaids were very good, and only started to cry again when they were out. There were ten of them in all, their skins various pretty shades of green, blue and violet, with tails and hair to match.

"We didn't realise it was a net," they sobbed. "It only looked like seaweed, boo–hoo!"

The Prince and Gemant comforted them and

helped them into the boulders where they could hide.

"We'll have to carry them down the cliff and back to the sea," said the Prince, wishing their tails weren't so heavy. "And what about *him*? He'll catch a whole lot more in a minute."

At that moment there was an angry cry from the depths of the basket.

"What about *me*?"

"We've missed one!" cried Gemant.

They ran back and stared down.

"I can't see anything – she ought to be green or blue, and glittery like the others. Wait – there's something red—"

"Of course there is," snapped the cross voice. "It's me, you stupid creature."

The Prince scowled.

"I think I know who *that* is," he said slowly. "It's your sister Gemael."

Gemant gave a cry of joy, reached into the basket, and pulled Gemael up in his arms without any help, he was so pleased.

Gemael didn't seem surprised to see Gemant. She gave him a brisk hug, took out a pocket comb and began to tidy her long black hair. Then from the same pocket she took the gold beetles the Prince remembered and began to clip them on to the strands with efficient crisp little snaps.

"I've had an awful time getting here," she said. "All that trouble and then getting stuck somewhere for simply ages and then whirling through and landing in the sea, *and* in a net with a lot of screaming mermaids."

Gemant tried to persuade her to come into the boulders and hide in case the Kreeler turned round, but instead Gemael jumped down from the basket, and ran straight up to him.

Appalled, Gemant and the Prince watched the tiny red figure standing behind the giant.

"You should be ashamed of yourself," she was yelling at him. A whirling appeared in the air beside her, and out of it she snatched a sword of white metal with rubies in the hilt.

"That's just like that silly sword she gave me to fight the Dragon of Brass with," said the Prince, dazed.

Gemael seized it with both hands, and threw it at the Kreeler.

With a terrific yell he leaped up – it probably felt like a wasp sting – and, losing his balance, fell over the cliff and down into the deep grey sea. Not that it would have seemed so deep to him, and the Prince waited anxiously for him to reappear. But he didn't. After a time the huge waves he had caused died down.

"Well," said Gemael, marching back along the cliff, "that's the end of *him*."

"How brave you were," said Gemant fondly.

"Ever since," said Gemael, "I had to help that stupid Prince deal with that Dragon I haven't been scared of a thing."

The Prince bristled. Gemael hadn't noticed him, and he was just going to stride up to her and say, "Oh, yes?" when she added more gently, "Though he *was* special, even if he was stupid. I don't know why."

"He's the Looked-for Deliverer," said Gemant.

"Oh, that must be the reason then," said Gemael. "Somehow I haven't stopped thinking about him since I whirled away and left him in the courtyard at the Castle of Bone. I wonder where he is?"

"Here," said the Prince.

Gemael gave a little jump, and then blushed. When this happened the Prince suddenly thought how lovely she was even though she was so cross and unreasonable, and how glad he was she had arrived at last, even though she would probably be very bossy and an awful nuisance. Then she stopped blushing, stamped her foot and growled at him, "It's rude to listen to what people are saying when they don't know you are."

And the Prince decided she wasn't lovely at all, and he wasn't glad she was there.

But Gemant was in high spirits.

"First we must take the mermaids back to the sea, and then we must have a party. Gemael, you'll say a spell for some food, won't you?"

At which the Prince decided he *was* glad she was there after all.

CHAPTER THIRTEEN

By the Sea

By the time they had carried all the mermaids down and found a dry piece of shore, the stars were coming out in the pale indigo sky. At least it had stopped raining.

Gemael muttered magic words and out of the air whirled a scarlet pavilion with an open front facing the sea, a beautiful warm fire, chairs, and a table with a damask cloth covered with steaming dishes of delicious food and gold jugs of wine. The Prince was rather impressed.

The mermaids and several sea-horses sat at the waves' edge and arranged some brightly coloured luminous fish just under the water to give extra light. They joined in the feast, and neighed and giggled and splashed because of the wine, and sang strange sea-songs about sunken ships and coral castles. Altogether it was a very happy party.

When the oval moon rose, Gemant turned to Gemael.

"You never did tell us, though, why you wanted to follow us. Were you bored with being the Lady of the Waste?"

Gamael frowned.

"It is a gruesome tale," said she.

Gemant and the mermaids looked very interested. The Prince pretended he wasn't.

Gemael began in her best gruesome-tale-teller's voice.

"When the Castle of Bone had fallen, and the Looked-for Deliverer had gone on his way to the mountains, Ysome's Skolks wandered in the Waste howling, and I was very glad. The days passed, as they had always done. But there was a sense of waiting and of disaster to come. And then—" Gemael paused dramatically, "—four nights before this night – there came a terrible humming from the sky and from the mountains. A grey glow shone beyond the peaks, and then there was the sound of a great rending – and – *It* came!!!"

"What?" cried the terrified mermaids and the disturbed Gemant.

Gemael, who had gone rather white, whispered, "*Nulgrave.*"

The mermaids sank back in terror, and the luminous fish dimmed.

The Prince thought Gemael was overacting, and had probably imagined it anyway, and he was annoyed because it had been such a good party until she had frightened everyone.

"However," went on Gemael, recovering herself, "I scorned to stay in the Waste and perish. I willed myself to the side of Gemant my brother in the oak wood – and it was very difficult because of the power of—of—what had come. But I did it. I, to whom magic is an open book – and then you weren't there," she added accusingly. Gemant began to apologise, but Gemael, ignoring him, went on, "Then I simply tried to will myself to wherever you might be, but it was hard, and the – *power* – was creeping over the mountains, and I thought I should be no more.

113

And in the midst of my trials I found myself in a No-Place – that is a place that is neither in this world, nor out of it. It was dark and silent, and strange winds blew. There I sat for longer than I knew, in despair. And then I found I could whirl again, and broke through into the daylight – and into the net of the Kreeler!"

The mermaids and the sea-horses applauded at this point because Gemael had got rid of the Kreeler.

"The Mad Witch put you into the No-Place," said Gemant, and explained how they had toiled for her so that she would help Gemael. Gemael didn't seem grateful, only rather annoyed she hadn't been able to whirl through on her own. Gemant also told her of Ysome's part in the story – Gemael glared and clenched her small fists at the very mention of Ysome's name – and spoke of the Grey Magic.

"Yes. She would. No wonder *It* broke through."

"Just what *is* Grey Magic?" asked the Prince.

"You really *don't* know anything, do you?" said Gemael rudely. "All of us who learn spells know *how* to work Grey Magic. It's the magic you call up when you stop wanting ever to do anything for anyone else – because you care only for yourself and what you can get for yourself, and it helps you. But in its way Grey Magic is a part of—of—the thing that came into the Waste, and so no one with any sense would ever *dream* of using it. But, of course, Ysome would. And, as *Nulgrave* was near and wanting to come into the world, Grey Magic turned the key and opened the door to it."

"And what *is* Nulgrave?" asked the Prince, feeling he was asking for the nine-hundredth time.

"I don't know," said Gemael simply.

114

The Prince would have liked to be sarcastic, but he felt altogether too anxious and scared. He got up and paced about.

"If you ask me, it's all ridiculous," he said angrily. "After all, look at it. I arrive here – not knowing who I am or where I come from. Gemael appears and tells me to go to the Castle of Bone and gives me a sword to fight the Dragon of Brass. Why? Because she wants to upset Ysome. I destroy the Dragon with Gemael's sword, the castle falls, and Ysome goes off and gets captured by the Purple Knight and then makes friends with him and lives in his tower. Then Gemant wants to rescue her, and we arrive, and because of us – of me – the Honnerdrin wood comes and stamps until the tower falls. Ysome is furious, and works Grey Magic to get even with me. Because of Grey Magic, Nul—well, the *Thing* gets into the world. Now, I'm supposed to be the Looked-for Deliverer who's going to deliver everybody from the *Thing*. And it's *because* of me, in a way, that *It*'s come."

There was a miserable silence, which was abruptly broken by a most terrifying bang in the distance.

Everyone jumped up in alarm.

"What is it? Where was it?" they cried.

And then, up over the line of cliffs, sprang a lurid yellow glare, as if a huge unhealthy fire were burning there. Other explosions followed the first, and a weird metallic grinding like rusty wheels.

The mermaids and sea-horses and fish dived into the water and swam down deep to hide.

Gradually the light and the noises faded.

But as they stared into the dark where they had been, a fourth moon rose into the sky.

"Horse," said the Prince, "you said there were only

three moons, and none of them was round."

"There are," said the horse-lion, "and none of them is."

"Now," said the Prince, "there's a fourth moon, and it *is* round."

It hung in the sky, distant but troubling. And the Prince's heart throbbed heavily because he knew – as he had known about the Castle of Bone, the mountains, the Knight's tower and the sea – he *had* to go on towards that frightful new moon and the place under it where the light and the bangs had been. He didn't want to go, would do anything not to have to.... And yet he did have to go. And that was that.

They spent an uneasy night. In the grey dawn, the Prince rose and started to walk up the shore alone, though rather noisily. After a minute there was a yell, and Gemant came running after him.

"Where are you going?"

"I've got to go – up there, where there was all that noise last night. I don't think you ought to come. You've got Gemael to worry about now."

"Oh, Gemael's very brave. I'd never forgive myself if I didn't go with you. After all, you are the Looked-fo—"

"Yes, yes. But – oh, well," said the Prince, who was glad they were going to come because it seemed less scaring if you didn't have to face danger on your own. The horse also appeared, looking like a horse.

"You have to take me, anyway," it said. "You're supposed to ride on me. Get up."

Then Gemael came and began to arrange everyone.

She said a spell for two coal-black horses for Gemant and herself – they had trappings of scarlet and gold – and a magic sword for Gemant.

"Be careful," the Prince warned him. "It won't cut through a thing."

"Oh, you don't cut with them," said Gemant, "you throw them."

"And then you're left with no sword."

"Oh, no, if you need them again they come straight back."

Soon they were galloping bravely up the stony beach and riding along the cliff. The ground was bare and rocky, but the day was warmer than before, and below, the sea was bluish mauve and very bright.

It seemed to be a long journey. At noon they rested and Gemael said a spell for lunch. While they were eating a shadow fell over the table. They looked up and saw a huge bird wheeling high in the sky on silent wings.

"Is it watching us?" asked Gemant.

The bird circled and dropped lower. And lower still. It had a wicked hooked red beak and black cruel eyes. Gemael stood up and said some magic at it. The bird gave a ghastly cry, but, instead of vanishing or just flapping off, it dived suddenly at the Prince, seized a strand of his hair and pulled it out. It then flew off with its prize, making hideous, pleased noises.

The Prince was fed up – he'd only taken his helm off a moment before.

"Perhaps it wanted it for its nest," said Gemant, but the Prince was certain the bird had had other, nastier reasons.

On that particular evening, the sun decided to sink behind them – in the same place it had risen. They found themselves riding through a skeletal wood of dead trees, and beyond the wood, the land stretched downwards to a bay. The tide had drawn out from this bay, the water like blood in the sunset, and the wet sand stretched out to an island of rock thrust up from the sea. On the island was an incredible yet familiar sight.

"The Castle of Bone!" cried the Prince, but he was wrong.

It wasn't simply a castle, it was a whole city this time that seemed to be built entirely of the bones of colossal ancient monsters – bone towers and ribcage walls and vertebrae palisades, skull palaces and dinosaur-pelvis stairs. If the Prince had been in any doubt – which he wasn't – the saffron flags flapping over the roofs and the black things flapping round the flags would have told him that Ysome was here.

"How did she—?" he began.

"With Grey Magic, she could do almost anything," said Gemael. "Even put a new moon into the sky."

She pointed, and they gazed upwards. There, floating over the City of Bone was the round white moon they had seen the night before. And it was indeed the strangest moon of all the strange moons, because it was a big white clock face with gold numbers round it and a pair of ornate black hands.

"What time does it say?" whispered Gemant.

"Seven o'clock," said the horse. "Which is quite correct."

And as the hands touched seven, the clock moon struck seven times with a thin cold chime.

CHAPTER FOURTEEN

Clock Moon

There was nothing the Prince would have liked better than to say, "Let's wait until morning." Hadn't Gemael, after all, once said that Ysome's power was greater by night? And he knew perfectly well that Ysome – somehow understanding that he would come this way (or had she even magicked him into coming this way?) – was waiting for him and plotting revenge. Perhaps even the feeling he had that he *must* get into the city was Ysome's magic, but he felt it wasn't.

"We must go across now," he said. "The tide's bound to be as silly as everything else here, and so goodness knows when it'll go out far enough again for us to reach the island. I say 'us'," he added nervously, "but really – I don't want to – but I ought to go alone."

"Not without me to ride," said the horse. "It would look wrong."

"I'll fight beside you to the death!" said Gemant.

Gemael glanced at the Prince scornfully.

"On your own? Don't be stupid. You'd only make a mess of everything as usual."

The Prince got annoyed, and feeling less terrified because he was annoyed, he urged the horse out across the sand.

He reached the rock first, and rode up it. He came

to a huge gate that seemed to be made out of pointed teeth, and realised he already didn't know what to do.

Gemael rode past him and pointed at the door.

"Jewelstar! Fly open bars!" she cried.

The Prince started. He suddenly remembered how the armies had cried "Jewelstar!" in the cup-picture the Theel had shown him.

"What's Jewelstar?" he asked her.

"Never mind," said Gemael. She obviously didn't know either.

The doors shuddered, and slid open a yard or so.

"Now!" cried Gemael.

They rode through, and the doors struggled out of the spell, closed again and relocked themselves, shutting the Prince and his companions into the city.

The streets of the city seemed deserted, and none of the palaces had any lamps in them. Thick darkness was falling, and soon the only light came from the great clock moon hanging overhead. They dismounted.

"Where now?" asked Gemant.

"I don't know. I—" the Prince broke off, listening. "Quick!"

They fled into a shadowy doormouth, and only just in time. Twenty large figures in iron armour and brass helmets came marching up the street, and turned out to be Beezles. They looked neither left nor right, but they carried burning torches, and axes. The Prince had an unpleasant feeling that they might be looking for something. However, they went past without stopping, and round a corner. When the heavy footfalls had died away they ventured out again.

"I think," said the Prince, "I have to go this way."
He set off up the street, the others close behind.

They moved on for a long while, once or twice seeing bands of marching Beezles, but always managing to hide in time. The Prince wished he knew where he was going. Finally they went up some steps, through a door, and he knew they were there. It was a circular room with many windows that looked out over the city. The Prince peered from each, and stared all round. Thunder sounded in the distance.

"I know it's here – but where is it, whatever it is?"

"Look up," said the horse.

They all did. Instead of a roof, the room was open to the sky, except where it was crossed over by four metal chains joined together in the middle. And from the middle a fifth chain of brass, each link as large as a cartwheel, started up into the night towards the spot where the clock moon hovered.

"The moon is anchored to the city by that chain," said the horse.

"Really?" said the Prince. "But why is that—"

There was an interruption, a distant noise that seemed to be coming closer and sounded like the baying of Skolks.

"Outside," cried the Prince, "or we'll be trapped in here."

They ran out, and down the steps. Overhead the clock moon struck eight, and suddenly a thousand lights appeared in the city, burning out of every palace window, every arch and doorway, blinding them. From each end of the street came pouring a horde of armoured Beezles with torches, and over the roofs and walls came packs of snuffling slavering

Skolks, and a flapping fog of Oggrings.

"Surprise! Surprise!' screamed countless spiteful voices.

Before he could even draw his sword the Prince was grabbed by strong relentless arms, and saw Gemant and Gemael also grabbed. They were then borne away up the brightly-lit streets.

The Prince didn't remember much of that journey. It was all a horrible blur of being dragged and prodded, of Skolks nipping at him whenever they got the chance – which was often – and Oggrings beating round his head.

Eventually he was pulled up an ornate staircase and through doors of gold and brass into an enormous hall with bone pillars, and blazing with fierce yellow light. Golden cobweb draperies hung from the walls and the chandeliers were set with golden glowworms. At the far end of the hall on a golden throne sat Ysome the Saffron in yellow silk and ermine, with a tall crown on her fair hair, guarded by twenty skeletons in gold armour leaning on brass axes.

Ysome waved a gracious hand.

"Welcome to my City of Clock Moon, sir Prince. I've been expecting you. One of my watch birds brought me this," she held up the piece of hair the bird had pulled out earlier in the day, "so I knew you were on your way. Do make yourself comfortable. You may throw him down here," she added.

And the Prince found himself thrown at her feet. He was bound hand and foot and hadn't even noticed before. Of Gemael and Gemant there was no sign.

"Where are my friends?" croaked the Prince, "and my horse?"

"In one of my nicest dungeons," said Ysome,

sweetly. "And now, dear Prince, I expect you'd like to know what's in store for you."

"No," said the Prince.

"I'm really very grateful to you." said Ysome. "You gave me the idea of working Grey Magic. I can't think why I never did before. And so, as a reward, I'm going to let you meet an old friend."

The skeletons chuckled and the Prince's blood ran cold.

Ysome rose, came down the steps and, once the Beezles had hauled the Prince to his feet and unbound him, took his arm in a friendly way. The Prince shuddered.

"Dear me, are you cold? Never mind, a little exercise is very warming."

In this manner they went out of the hall and up more stairs, the guards giving the Prince an occasional prod and punch to help him on his way. He wondered wildly if he could seize Ysome and hold his sword to her throat and so escape while the skeletons and Beezles were too afraid for her safety to attack him. But his sword seemed to have gone, and, anyway, he had a feeling that if he did she would say some sort of spell at him that would turn him into stone or something like that.

Then they emerged into the open on to a bone walk lit by flaring torches. The walk surrounded a huge courtyard below that somehow looked familiar.

"You may choose a weapon," said Ysome.

"Why?"

"I like to see things done fairly. Now. Sword, axe or spear?"

"I'd like my own sword back," said the Prince, trying not to panic.

"Ah, no," Ysome tinkled. "That was the sword

Vultikan the Hoiler made you, and we all know *that* can cut through anything. It will have to be an ordinary sword, I'm afraid. And remember, the foolish Lady of the Waste won't be able to help you now."

A Skolk ran up with a sword in its mouth. Ysome patted it, took the sword and held it out to the Prince. Even in his terror, he could see it was very blunt.

"I've changed my mind, I'd like an axe—"

"Oh, much too late. Only one choice, my dear. Down to the courtyard!"

About fifty Oggrings whizzed at the Prince, seized various bits of his clothing and of him in their teeth, and flew him down to the court, where they dropped him with a bump.

The Prince picked himself up. Thunder sounded very near, and a bright grey lightning flared overhead. His visor fell down over his face.

And then came a sound the Prince remembered only too well.

"It can't be. I shorted it," he wailed to himself, staring at the great widening black crack in the far wall. "And Vultikan wouldn't mend it, so it *can't* be—" but he remembered Ysome had worked Grey Magic, and with this power could do almost anything. Rusty smoke filled the court, and there came again the grinding of metal cogs. The wall opened wide, and through it, the light spilling on its brazen flanks, empty eyes burning, nostrils steaming, came the Dragon of Brass. It was just as terrible as he recalled, only now it seemed bigger, stronger, and, as it opened its appalling hinged jaws, he saw the metal mesh across its throat. No one would be able to throw a sword down into it this time.

The Prince backed away, and the Dragon came

plodding after him, its joints screeching.

The Prince ran at the Dragon and hit it with the sword, which immediately snapped off at the hilt. Cheers came from the wall.

The Prince ran back.

"Perhaps if I could hit one of its eyes—?" He judged, balanced the hilt and threw it. It missed, glanced off the Dragon's crest and fell out of sight in the shadows. "It's useless," thought the Prince, near to tears of fright, anger and despair. "Oh, I'm sorry, Gemant and Gemael and horse and everyone. But it'll all be over in a few minutes, and there's nothing I can do."

And he stopped running away and stood quite still, and stared at the Dragon defiantly.

"Go on, then, do your worst. And I hope I choke you."

The Dragon, however, instead of coming on at him, suddenly stopped, and reared up its head at the sky. In the silence the Prince heard for the first time a horrible, thin, high-pitched hum. It seemed to come from above, and yet he felt it all around him. Confusion broke out on the wall. Skolks howled mournfully and Oggrings sank down in heaps. Ysome began to call out spells that apparently didn't work.

And then there was a noise – a sound like tearing paper except that it was much louder – and the sky was as bright as day.

"*Nulgrave!*" whispered the Prince.

For a moment he stood still, not knowing what to do. Then he realised that the Dragon seemed to be frozen to the spot, its head still craning at the sky, and that in the confusion on the wall no one was taking any notice of him. A shuddering ran through the ground, and he heard a tower fall somewhere in the City of Bone. He thought of Gemael and Gemant and the horse in the dungeons, and he ran past the Dragon, through the open wall and down a dark corridor.

Turning a corner he found a frightened skeleton.

"Which way to the dungeons?" cried the Prince.

The skeleton pointed with a trembling fingerbone.

Down and down ran the Prince until he found himself in a gloomy hall. At the hall's centre was an open well in the floor. As he peered into it, a voice said, "We're all here." It was the horse. "We're in a net," it went on, "and there's a rope attached to a pulley in the corner. If you turn the handle it will wind up the rope and lift us out."

The Prince ran to look for the pulley and collided with it. He got up again, turned the handle frantically, and panted, because it was hard work. Finally the heads of three horses and Gemael and Gemant appeared over the top of the well. They scrambled out.

"I would have thought you could have said a spell or something," puffed the Prince to Gemael.

"No magic would work now," said Gemael. "*It*'s here."

The ground shook under their feet. Thunder sounded, and again the tearing noise came, louder than at first.

"What next?" asked the Prince.

A silence fell. There seemed to be nowhere else to run to.

"I suggest—" said the horse.

"Yes? Yes?"

"We climb the brass chain to the clock moon."

Immediately they flew from the dungeon hall, up stairs, through doors, out into the streets, following the horse, who seemed to remember the way back. As they ran it occurred to the Prince what a silly idea it was that they climb the brass chain of the clock. In any case, where could it lead to apart from the open sky? But any idea was as good as another in this dreadful mess of a world.

"Here we are!" cried Gemant.

They had managed to get on to the edge of the open roof where the five chains were joined together. The Prince stared back over the city. Many palaces had fallen, but the sky was dark again overhead. A sort of fog seemed to be creeping towards them, and the Prince didn't like the look of it.

"Well, for a start," said the Prince, "how are the horses going to climb the chain?"

"They're magic horses," said Gemael. "They can do all sorts of things."

"I'll go first," said Gemant, "in case there's – anything – at the top."

He began to scale the chain as if it were a ladder, and the two black horses followed him, managing amazingly well with their hooves.

"You go next," said the Prince to Gemael, who looked pale and terrified.

"Oh, I'm not afraid," said she, scurrying after the horses.

The white horse turned into a lion and leaped after her, and the Prince went last. He wasn't sure how this had happened, nor that he really wanted to go last.

Looking back as they climbed he saw a black swirling smoke coiling round tower after tower, and wondered if something were on fire.

It was very silent then except for the scrape of hooves and feet and claws on the brass chain of the clock.

CHAPTER FIFTEEN

The Palace in the Clouds

To the Prince it seemed they had been climbing for hours. The ground, which was now a long way below, was completely in darkness; not a light showed. They, on the other hand, were climbing up into the bright white glare of the clock moon which loomed enormously above them. The Prince squinted at it, and suddenly saw to his horror that the hands were just about to touch nine o'clock. The chime had sounded loud from the ground. Now they were so close to it, they would be deafened.

He looked wildly around him for escape. There wasn't one.

"Horse!" he cried, but in that moment the first stroke came. The Prince felt sure it was striking in his head, it was so loud and awful. He lost all sense of where he was, clapped his hands over his ears, and next second was falling downwards into the darkness.

"Help!" he tried to scream.

Then the next stroke sounded and blotted out even fear with its noise.

All around was soft stuff that felt rather like several furry quilts piled on top of each other. The Prince sat up and stared about him. It was dark, but with tufts of pale-blue light everywhere that the Prince didn't understand.

"Help?" he asked.

Had he fallen into Clock Moon and been killed? He only remembered hearing two strokes of the frightful clock, and then—

A heaving and ruffling began to happen in the tufts in front of him. Suddenly something shoved its way through. Thinking it might be a monster of some sort – it usually had been up to now – the Prince jumped up and tried to draw his sword. While he was remembering he no longer had one he discovered that the thing in the hole was a pale face with black hair round it.

"Gemael!" he cried. "Wherever are we? What happened?"

Gemael floundered the rest of the way through the fluffy stuff which separated them.

"We all fell off the clock chain," she said unhappily. "The noise was so awful and the chain shook so. And now – I think we fell into a cloud."

"What? All of us?"

"No," Gemael wailed. "I don't know where Gemant is, or the horses. I couldn't find you for ages." And she burst into tears.

The Prince wasn't certain if she were crying over not being able to find him or because she *had* found him. Deciding it was the first, he put his arm round her.

"There, there," he said, and became quite fond of her, since comforting her took his mind off his own worries.

As they sat on the fluffy stuff, however, he had a feeling that the cloud, if it *was* a cloud, was moving.

And then, not long after he had felt this, the cloud seemed to stop still.

"I wonder where we are now?" he asked.

Gemael dried her eyes and began to comb her hair.

"You should go out and see," she said sternly. "Here's a magic sword," and she produced one from the air.

The Prince took the sword and, filled with misgivings, tugged away at the wall of the cloud until he had made a sizeable gap. He peered out and saw only limitless blackness.

"I think, wherever we are, we ought to wait until it gets light," he told Gemael. But Gemael had fallen fast asleep. The Prince, very relieved, pulled the cloud together again, and lay down to do the same. The last thing he heard as the cloud-warmth lulled him into dreams was a distant tinkling sound.

He woke up because it was dawn, and somehow he seemed to be in the centre of it. Opening his eyes he saw that the cloud was no longer dark, but amber, pink and gold. He pulled open the sides of it again, and what was outside was so lovely he couldn't possibly be afraid.

They were in the sky, and the sky was golden streaked with silver thread like a tapestry. In front and away stretched a floor of clouds that were bronze, lilac and emerald, with pools of rose-red fire in them that must have been reflections of the sun. In the far distance stood up cloud-shapes like mountains, all soft purple, and on these stood the sun itself. And of all the amazing things the sun was the most amazing, for it was simply enormous and must be very near. It blazed like a diamond doughnut, but was no more bright than it had seemed from the ground, and gave only a pleasant warmth. The Prince was astonished. This close, he thought, it should have scorched them all up. But then, this silly sun wasn't a bit like the sun where *he* came from – wherever that was. You couldn't get anywhere near *his* sun.

He found Gemael was standing beside him.

"We're in the Cloud Lands," she said, "where the Sky People come from."

"Is that good?" asked the Prince.

Gemael stepped past him and out of the cloud. Although her feet seemed to sink a little way into the coloured mist, she didn't fall through. The Prince joined her. It was like walking in feathers.

"Look!" cried Gemael.

The Prince swung round in fright, clutching the magic sword. Behind the cloud, which was now lifting and drifting away, was an empty silver chariot drawn by two silver horses. They nodded at the Prince, and the crystals chinked on their bridles.

"We're meant to get in," said Gemael, and did so.

The Prince followed her, rather more slowly, and next minute the horses were leap-flying along about six feet above the clouds, flapping their fiery wings.

"Where are they taking us?" worried the Prince.

Neither Gemael nor the silver horses answered. They seemed to be making towards the purple mountains. Then they went down over a little dip into a lagoon of soft flame, and in the near distance stood an incredible building that looked as if it were made of green ice. As they got nearer there was a break in the cloud below, and pale sky showed through. The Prince thought the sky was rather like a moat of water around the green building, which seemed to be a palace of some sort. Sure enough, just then, a

132

rainbow appeared over the sky-moat – a drawbridge. As they crossed it, the Prince peered down, but could see nothing of the ground, only some cloudlets swimming about like fish. And then they were off the rainbow, through a sparkling green arch, and into a vast hall with an open roof. The horses stopped.

The Prince felt embarrassed, because the hall was full of people who all seemed to be looking at him. Every so often a cloud would drift through the hall and out of the open roof, and partly because of this the Prince found it hard to see these people properly. Another thing was that they were all rather transparent like the two he had found in the chariot on the heath, and they were all very beautiful. Their long cloudy hair was every colour the clouds could be, and their rainbow clothes confused him, and they were extremely quiet. He recalled that the horse had said they never talked, and wondered if they would all stand there for ever, gazing at him and not saying anything.

But just as he was starting to go hot and cold, a man and a woman came through the cloud drifts up to the chariot. His hair was red like a sunset, hers apple green. They smiled at the Prince.

"You are very welcome," they murmured as one.

"The horse said you never talked," blurted the Prince.

"The horse often tells lies," said the woman, laughing. "Hadn't you noticed?"

"Well, now you come to mention it," said the Prince.

Just then he caught sight of a lion nodding modest agreement behind the chariot. Gemant and the two black horses were embracing Gemael.

"We fell into *another* cloud," Gemant was explaining.

The Prince got down from the chariot, and the red-haired man and apple-haired woman each took one of his arms. This made the Prince feel very happy, he wasn't certain why.

"We have much to tell you," said the man gently, "and we must be swift, because there isn't much time. My name is Themon."

"But first you must be hungry and thirsty," added the woman. "And my name is Themistra."

"You don't happen to know *my* name?" said the Prince.

"You are the Looked-for Deliverer."

"I was afraid I was."

They took him to a beautiful green-ice balcony which overlooked the cloud mountains. The cloud colours were changing all the time as the sun rolled slowly by overhead, and now everything was gold and blue and peach. The Prince sipped something that looked like mist out of a crystal goblet. It tasted delicious and satisfied both hunger and thirst. He wasn't sure where Gemant, Gemael and the horses were, but he knew they would be all right with the Sky People.

"You see," Themon said to him after a while, as if continuing an earlier conversation, "the laws of our world are quite different from those of the world you come from. They probably seem to make no sense to you at all."

"They don't," admitted the Prince.

"And that is the very reason," said Themon, "why only someone from another world could save us from the threat of Nulgrave. Although many things seem

134

baffling and silly to you, certain dangers which would overcome someone who didn't think them baffling cannot harm *you* in the end."

"They still frighten me," said the Prince.

"That's different, and doesn't matter at all."

"For many thousands of years," went on Themistra, pouring the Prince more mist, "Nulgrave has waited around the borders of our world, ready to pounce. As time went by, resistance to Nulgrave grew weaker, and finally it only needed Grey Magic to open the door. But we have always known One would come who could fight Nulgrave, and win, as none of our world could. You are that One. The way you have already got the better of the Bezzles, Ysome, the Dragon of Brass, the Honnerdrin, the Purple Knight, the Mad Witch, the chiming clock moon – show that you are He."

"But I didn't – I mean, half the time it was some crazy mistake or accident, or someone else did something – not me."

"That is not the point," said Themon. "It was your *influence* – because you were *there* – that things went the way they should."

"Oh," said the Prince. He thought a moment. "Where is Nulgrave now?" he asked in a small voice.

Themon led him to the rail of the balcony and they looked down into the sky-moat. Themon murmured some strange words, and there was a sort of swirling below. Suddenly the clear brightness was gone. The Prince found he was staring down at the earth far beneath. But he couldn't see it very well. Here and there the top of a tower or a tall tree poked out, but mostly everything was smothered by a dark coiling *something* – like a poisonous fog. The Prince turned away and Themon said the spell to shield the sky again.

"Is it all — covered by — *that*?" asked the Prince.

"Yes. And soon, unless it is stopped, Nulgrave will rise to the Cloud Lands and there will be darkness everywhere."

"But what can *I* do?" cried the Prince in familiar panic.

"You can lead us all against it. Teach us how to fight it."

"But I don't even know what it is — it looks like smoke to me, how do you fight that?"

"Ah," said Themon, "I'd forgotten that you don't understand yet what Nulgrave *is*."

"Do *you*?" gasped the Prince.

"Do you remember times," said Themistra, "when you were truly unhappy? When nothing you could think of to do, nowhere you could think of to go, were worth it: when nothing could cheer you, and everything seemed quite useless and pointless, when each day was miserable and the next day was the same? Then you would simply sit and be sad, and it seemed you could never be anything *but* sad. Well, that is what Nulgrave is — only worse, far worse. Nulgrave is Despair."

"And if anyone from our world is enclosed by Tarshish, they become despairing and their lives waste away until they die," added Themon.

"Then I don't see what I can do!" almost shouted the Prince.

"You don't belong to our world," said Themon, smiling. "To you Tarshish will be a black smoke, an unpleasant prickly cold. You will fear it, yes. But it won't make you *feel* any different from the way you

136

have always felt. You *won't* despair. And because of that you can help others to fight, for that is the only way to drive Nulgrave out – to *fight* it with happiness, to *fight* it by not caring about it or what it can do."

Themon took the Prince's left hand, Themistra took his right. They led him from the balcony into another great hall, and here waited rank upon rank of shining men and women mounted on silver horses.

"We are the first part of your army," said Themon.

A thousand glittering swords flashed in the air, and multi-hued banners fluttered. Suddenly the Prince felt warm and relaxed. A lump came into his throat, but he cleared it and cried out, "Jewelstar forever!"

And the shout echoed back to him from the Sky People, strong and unafraid.

The Prince looked at Themistra and asked very low, "What's Jewelstar?"

"Joy," said Themistra, and laughed joyfully.

CHAPTER SIXTEEN

The Battle against Darkness

Down the sky they whirled!

It was exciting and strange. They passed a huge, dim, pale shape, which was the square moon without its night-light on, and several crystal castles floated by on apricot clouds. The Prince was delighted that they had somehow given his horse a pair of fiery wings so that it too could flap through the air like all the others.

But the delight soon faded. It got dull and dark, and there below lay the black smoke clouds which were Nulgrave.

The Prince swallowed nervously.

"Courage, horse!" he cried.

"I'm not bothered," said the horse. "I've been with you so long I doubt if I shall despair either."

Themon and Themistra rode to the Prince's side in their chariot, and the horse slowed.

"We can go no further for the present," said Themon.

"What? But I thought you were coming with me."

"We shall – but we can't face Nulgrave until you have gone down first and exerted your influence over it." The Prince scowled, but Themistra leaned out and handed him a beautiful silver trumpet. "Sound this, and we shall come to fight the battle with you."

"Thank you," said the Prince, feeling they had led him up the garden path rather. "Well . . . I'll see you later then. If I make it, that is."

Themon and Themistra beamed at him, and so did Gemant and Gemael, who were also showing no signs of following. The Prince glared at them all, and told the horse to carry on down.

"Well, I like that." He grumbled, "They all said they'd stick by me to the end and all that, and then they just leave me to it."

"Oh," said the horse, "they'll come after you, but if they came now Nulgrave would overwhelm them."

"It may overwhelm me," muttered the Prince.

And then the darkness seemed to rise to meet them, black vapour swirled round them, and they were into the heart of the evil thing.

The Prince looked round in horror, but, before he could decide if he was despairing or not, some of the stuff went down the wrong way and he had a coughing fit, sneezed a couple of times, blew his nose and cursed energetically. After which he realised he wasn't despairing, and, although it was rather cold and foggy and he couldn't see very well, he was neither miserable nor scared. Just then they collided with the top branches of a dead tree. The horse's fiery wings set it alight, and the next moment they were bumping on to the ground.

The Prince picked himself up.

"Are you all right, horse?"

The horse turned into a lion and clawed twigs out of its mane.

"Yes," said the horse-lion. "I couldn't make out where we were going. And the tree did something to the wings and they vanished. However, the blazing wood gives quite enough light to see now, doesn't it?"

The horse didn't sound despairing either. Encouraged, the Prince peered ahead of him, and it seemed to him that the darkness was not so thick around them as it was everywhere else.

"Ho!!!" something roared through the fog.

The Prince yelled in fear, and realised he shouldn't have because the something bawled back, "I'm a-coming! Keep shouting, I'll find you."

"Help," said the Prince, "let's run!"

But it was too late. A large shape was striding towards them, howling out, "I see you!"

In the light of the burning tree the Prince discovered a tall, muscular giant with red, ragged hair, yellow eyes, and a bag of tools over his shoulder.

"Vultikan!"

"Who else?" bellowed Vultikan. He leaned down to the Prince and held out a gleaming sword with a dragon hilt. "Left this in the enchantress's bone city. Vultikan makes you a sword, and then you leave it behind," he added disgustedly.

"How did you know where it was?" asked the Prince. "And how did you know where *I* was?"

"Still asking his daft questions," Vultikan remarked to the horse-lion.

"He still doesn't properly understand," said the horse.

"I'd better tell him then. You can hold off Nulgrave," said Vultikan scathingly, "so everyone is going to sense where you are by the *feel* of the place. They'll all be here soon."

"Who will?" asked the Prince uneasily.

"Everyone." Vultikan sat on a boulder. "Hung on to your armour," he congratulated.

The tree-fire was dying down, and the Prince was

now certain that the darkness was drawing off from him, though it was just as thick a few yards away.

Vultikan broke alarmingly into song.

"Haven't felt like singing since Nulgrave came," he said after the third verse of something about hoiling and boiling and the mountain life, "but now you're back, well—"

"Er," said the Prince, trying to stop him from breaking out again, "who did you say was coming?"

Vultikan, however, had begun once more and wouldn't stop. He accompanied himself by banging his hammer on the boulder, and altogether he made a lot of noise. At least he seemed quite happy.

Suddenly the Prince's visor fell down with a crash. This always seemed to happen before some sort of fight or disaster, and the Prince became worried. The lion turned into a horse and said, "Get up on me now. It will look better."

The Prince started to argue, but then he realised he might be able to get away faster on the horse if anything dreadful occurred, so he mounted. Vultikan stopped singing, and in the quiet the Prince heard an alarming babble that seemed to be coming from below and yet was apparently getting closer by the second. It sounded like people crying and people shouting, and horses neighing and dogs barking and wheels grinding and bits of metal clanking. After a time the Prince could make out torches, smudged together by the fog into a dirty orange mist, crawling across some sort of valley beneath, and then up a slope that ran towards him.

It took about twenty minutes for the first people in the procession to reach him, but after that they arrived thick and fast. They were all sorts and shapes and sizes, wearing all kinds of strange clothes and weird armour, or what they thought might do for armour, such as iron buckets on their heads and silver dinner plates strapped over their chests. Some rode in wagons, some on horses, some walked. Most of them looked dreadfully miserable and were complaining or crying. Despite what Vultikan had said, and also the fact that they seemed to be dressed up for some sort of battle, they didn't appear to know why they'd come. They stood around, and a droning, mournful noise rose up from them like a thick cloud of wasps. It got darker.

"What shall I do with them?" muttered the Prince.

The horse pretended not to hear.

The Prince rode forward, and up and down the front of the crowd.

"I'm—er—the Looked-for Deliverer," he ventured.

They stared at him listlessly, all very pale, and too sad even to cry now.

"Nulgrave isn't so bad here," said the Prince jollily.

Some of them were almost transparent, like ghosts. The torches were fluttering out in their limp hands. He saw a woman in a green kirtle, and she looked like the one on the marsh who had thrown stones at him.

"Hallo again!" he cried cheerfully.

She gazed at him and heaved a melancholy sigh.

Just then there was an awful noise behind them. It was actually Vultikan sighing too. As if at a signal, the horse reared up in fright and the Prince rolled off its back. Falling with the usual crash and clatter, he didn't hear at first the titter which ran among the crowd. But as he struggled up he could see people at the front passing the word back about what had happened.

142

"I'm glad you think it's funny," said the Prince. "Well, I'm not doing it again just to make *you* laugh." At which he fell over a root. Roars of laughter. Scowling, the Prince got up once more. However, he was glad they looked more normal, and the darkness had drawn off again.

"Right!" he cried, "well, there's only one way to fight Nulgrave – and that's to be happy and occupied, so—er— Horse—?"

This time the horse had something to say.

"Party games," it said.

It really wasn't how the Prince had seen it at all. He'd thought it might be noble and dignified when you delivered people, but it wasn't. It meant groups yowling out songs and dancing ring-a-ring-a-roses, running races, having quizzes and asking each other totally silly-sounding questions (the Prince thought), and telling jokes. He considered it was all quite awful, but it certainly cheered them up, and it got lighter. In fact he could now see they were on some bunched-up hills, though the fog still circled round them about half a mile away on every side. They also built a bonfire, which kept everyone busy finding sticks, although Vultikan had done something to it so it couldn't go out unless he said so. Luckily there were some witches among the crowd who provided regular meals.

Three days passed in the hills, and all the while more people poured in. The Prince recognised the Purple Knight, looking sheepish with a group of Beezles riding on Drumbils, who all swore to follow the Prince to the death, which he didn't believe, and other things he didn't believe either. There were knights too he hadn't met, but who looked as if they'd have behaved just like the Purple Knight. Buzzles arrived and Bezzles – squeaking and looking spiteful but scared – and even some things with eight legs which the horse said were Bizzles. As each band of travellers came in they told of others they'd passed on the road, and the Prince heard with some alarm that they had seen a great oak wood marching in the distance.

"Perhaps they won't get here," he consoled himself. And they didn't.

On the fourth day it seemed as if everyone who was going to arrive had done so. There were tents every- where, and lots of mad games and noise.

"What happens now?" the Prince asked the horse.

"Post a look-out in that tree over there," said the horse.

"Why?"

"Because," said the horse.

The Prince did not want to send someone up the tree to be look-out because they would want to know what they were looking out for and he couldn't tell them, so he climbed up himself. It was a tall tree, and from the top he could see right out across the camp, over the hills, into the black fog that was Nulgrave. And something very odd was happening to Nulgrave. It was jetting up in great gusts, and cold little fires were jumping about in it. Soon he began to hear a thin, high-pitched hum. Down below, the people in the camp were making too much row with their quizzes and races to hear it. The Prince craned forward and almost fell out of the tree. Suddenly all the black smoke ran together and upwards into a towering, pitch-coloured pillar several miles high.

Then it seemed to coil round and round itself like a furious snake, gushed over the backs of the hills – and was gone.

"Jewelstar!" screamed the Prince, half scrambling, half falling down the tree trunk. "It's gone, it's run away – I never knew it would be so easy – all this talk about fighting, and this silly armour—"

He slid the last foot or so and landed on the horse's back.

"You don't understand," said the horse.

The Prince looked round, and saw that all the games and noise had stopped. Everyone looked very stern and purposeful, and they were buckling on extra dinner plates.

"Nulgrave hasn't run off," said the horse. "It's drawn all its strength together in one place. There's a large valley over there, and that's where it will be. Waiting for us."

"But can't we just – er – leave it there?"

"No," said the horse. "This is the last fight. Either It or we will perish."

"I see," said the Prince.

"So blow the silver trumpet Themistra gave you."

At first the Prince couldn't find it. Then he couldn't blow it. It felt like trying to blow up a balloon, which he had never been any good at either. In the end, Vultikan blew it, and the Prince went deaf in the left ear for ten minutes.

There was a sound of wings overhead, and out of the pale blue sky came flying the army of the Cloud Lands and Themon and Themistra in their chariot. The horses landed in a rainbow fire-blaze on the hills, and up galloped two black stallions with Gemael and Gemant. Gemant clasped the Prince's hand.

"I say, so good to see you again."

"What?" asked the Prince.

Gemant spoke in his right ear.

"This is it, then."

"Apparently," said the Prince, as if it were nothing to do with him.

"Now a witch must cast the runes."

"What? What have prunes got to do with it?"

Gemael leaned over and tapped the Prince's ear in an irritated way, after which the Prince found he could hear again.

"It's always done before a battle," said Gemant, "to make sure of victory."

The Prince didn't understand – he still thought Gemant had said something about prunes. But Gemael went up on to a little hillock where everyone could see her. She raised her arms and looked very impressive in all her scarlet, with her long black hair blowing in the wind.

"By Earth, by Air—" she began, and was promptly interrupted by a flash of green light. Out of the light jumped a thin figure with long thin arms, a wasp dress, a tide of fierce grey hair and a malicious grin.

"I am the Mad Witch!" it cried with glee, waving its staff which had a jade-green skull for a knob. "I've come to cast the runes! Ha! Nonsense!"

"I was here first," said Gemael with dignity.

"Rubbish," said the Witch, and obviously meant it.

"I—" began Gemael haughtily.

The Witch spun round on one foot in a gesture the Prince remembered too well. "Zellezor-in-Parrapax!" she yelled.

Poor Gemael made no further interruption as the Witch screamed her way through a lot of chants,

146

pointing East, West, North and South, occasionally crying "Nonsense!" and jumping in the air. When she finally stopped there was some polite applause.

"You'd better go and thank her," said Gemant. "And ask her to turn Gemael back, would you?" he added in a troubled voice.

Uneasily the Prince dismounted and walked up on to the hillock.

"Oh, it's you!" cried the Witch.

"Thanks for casting the prunes," said the Prince vaguely, looking round to see just where she'd cast them in case he trod on one, "and will you undo the spell on Gemael?"

"No. Stuck-up baggage! Do her good. Bah!" The Witch approached unpleasantly near and poked the Prince in the chest with a skinny finger. "I've got some news for you."

"What?"

"That Egg of yours I took—"

"The Egg— My secret—" cried the Prince, thinking she might be going to return it to him.

"Gone!" screamed the Witch delightedly.

"Gone where?"

"The Honnerdrin," said the witch, and hugged herself and grinned as if this explained everything.

"What do you mean?"

Themon came up beside the Prince.

"I'm afraid," he said, "the Witch has given the Egg to a marsh-snake to play with. Didn't you, Mad Witch?"

The Witch screamed with laughter and nodded violently several times.

"Only it wasn't a snake – it was a Honnerdrin in disguise."

"So now the Honnerdrin have got my secret – and they're my sworn enemies!"

Themon looked very serious.

"Not only that, I'm sorry to say. We watched all these things from the sky, and the last we saw of the Honnerdrin was the great oak wood marching into the very maw of Nulgrave, offering your Egg as a token of friendship if Nulgrave would spare them. It won't, of course, but it may use the Honnerdrin while it needs them. And the Egg."

The Prince felt frightened, and then furious. Despite her magic, he turned and glared at the Witch and took a menacing step towards her. At which the Witch shrieked, "Myself begone!" There was a green flash again, and no Witch.

"What am I going to *do*?" wailed the Prince. Then he folded his arms and said sternly, "I shall pretend it didn't happen. Horse!" The horse came up and the Prince remounted. The Prince raised his arm. "Jewelstar!" he roared.

At once the army roared back, "Jewelstar!"

The Prince felt better.

"Form up behind me," he cried, "and I shall lead you all into battle."

Everyone began to rush around and shout and get jumbled up. While they were doing this, the Prince leaned over and kissed the frozen Gemael gently on her cheek. He wasn't sure why he did. It just seemed the right thing to do.

"Don't worry, Gemael," he said. "The worst's happened, so things can only get better now. If I come back from the battle I'll release you from the spell somehow or other, I promise. If I don't come back and we lose – well. It won't really matter for very long if you're under a spell or not."

He looked away and blew his nose, and then noticed that the army was in place behind him.

"Forward!" cried the Prince. "And godspeed!"

"Jewelstar forever! Jewelstar undaunted!" shouted the armies.

"Right," said the Prince. "Come on, then, horse."

And the next second they were galloping, galloping, galloping over the hunch-backed hills, across the narrow ravines, towards the Valley of the Shadow where Nulgrave lay in wait.

In the bowl of the valley the dark thing rolled like ink.

It was like jumping forward down the steps into an old cellar – dark, cold, with no light anywhere except from the door behind you, and then the door slams shut, and there is no light at all. Thick, black, icy horror all around. A cry of terror went up from the army as they were flung down into it.

"Jewelstar!!!!" yelled the Prince, and the word seemed to give him unexpected strength.

He stared down at the horse and its eyes and nostrils were wide and red with fury as it dashed on. The Prince drew his sword and slashed left and right, not knowing if it did any good.

And then abruptly there was a kind of dim glow ahead, and in the glow stood up a mile-high solid wall that seemed to be made of stone. The army broke up in panic, veering left and right. But the Prince heard a faint, far-off rustling, like leaves, and he guessed.

"It's not real!" he cried out, "it's the Honnerdrin. Traitors!" he yelled and rode straight at the wall, wheeling his sword round and round his head, and stabbing into the stone, which groaned and fell apart and for a moment looked like trees, and then vanished. "Death to the traitors!" yelled the Prince. A battle-madness came on him so that he felt happy and strong and saw very little except a red mist in front of his eyes. Things loomed out of the mist and the blackness – giants, ogres, monsters with wings and teeth and lashing tails – and he cut them all down one after the other, not knowing if they were real, or the Honnerdrin, or part of Nulgrave itself. And the army, given great courage by the Prince's cries and brave actions, rushed after him and did as well as he did. Gemant slew seven fiends with live coals for eyes, who crashed down under his sword and became fallen oaks. The Purple Knight put paid to a dragon of flame which went out like a candle under his blade. Beezles and Bezzles and Buzzles lashed around them, Bizzles stamped, Drumbils reared and tore with their teeth, and Vultikan wielded his great hammer like an axe and felled twenty monsters in a neat row. There were even Skolks leaping on things, and Oggrings flapping at things, but there were no Theels, who were, as the horse had once remarked, "incapable of harming another".

The noise was incredible and frightful, and the blackness seemed all broken up in pieces.

And then the joy and anger faded out of the Prince, and he realised it was very quiet.

"That's odd," he said aloud, wondering if he had gone deaf again, but he hadn't. He found he was standing quite on his own – the horse had disappeared – and there wasn't a sound to be heard, not even a distant neigh or shout. The Prince felt nervous. He looked around him, and he was in a ghastly, ghostly oak wood, where all the trees were half transparent. It wasn't black, there was a sort of murky, iron-coloured light, shot through with lightning flickers. The Prince shivered. "I mustn't be afraid," he said to himself. "That's what it wants." So he started to whistle, but the whistling sounded eerie in the silence so he stopped. "Anyone in?" enquired the Prince, managing not to sound too scared. He started to saunter up an avenue of trees, hoping he might find a way out and back to the others. And then a voice came into his head, a sickening, dull, inhuman voice, and, although it didn't speak words, the Prince understood exactly what it said.

"You are finished. Despair. Despair and weep."

"No thank you," said the Prince, gritting his teeth.

"Despair and weep. Weep and die."

"Hasn't anyone told you," said the Prince, shaking from head to foot, "that I come from another world? You don't upset *me* out here in the back of beyond."

"You are afraid."

"Not really. I often tremble like this – it means I'm bored."

"You are afraid."

"Well, even if I were – which I'm not – I'm not in despair." And this was very true. He felt the dark thing recoil slightly, as if it understood. And then a small figure came running between the trees holding up something in one hand. The Prince felt relieved for a moment, and then he saw what it was. It was a thin, brown child with long, acorn-coloured hair and greenish-yellow eyes, regarding the Prince with an amused sneer, and grasping an egg.

The child halted a few feet away, and casually tossed the egg – which was *the* Egg – from hand to hand.

"Destroy the Egg."

The Prince jumped. He was horrified. If the Egg were destroyed he would never know who he really was—

"More than that," whispered the voice in his mind, *"if the Egg is destroyed before it hatches out – you will cease to exist."*

The Prince jumped again.

"A mere Honnerdrin couldn't break the shell," he muttered. "The Theel said it couldn't be broken until it was ready to hatch."

"It is about to hatch. It will be easy to crack and ruin."

The Prince stared at the Honnerdrin child, and the child said slowly, "I warned you Nulgrave was coming."

He realised it was the same child he and Gemant had seen by the ditch when the oak wood chased them on the heath.

In its hands the Egg seemed to move.

"Destroy the Egg. Destroy it."

The Honnerdrin child suddenly grinned.

"Honnerdrin," it said, "don't like obeying *anyone*. Catch!" And then it flung the Egg to the Prince.

With a yell the Prince leaped forward, grabbed at the Egg, dropped it, caught it again, and ended up on the ground clutching it in both hands. A great black wave came sweeping across the trees and the child vanished into it, but a bright crackling was coming from the Egg. Bits of shell burst out in all directions. A blue light glowed in the Prince's hands, took on for a moment the shape of a bird, and flew straight up at the Prince, and through his helm into his brain. The Prince gave a cry of pure joy. He leapt up and laughed. •

"Well, that fixes *you*," he yelled at the darkness, "because now I know who I am, where I came from and what I'm doing here. And I know that I'll win. There isn't any reason why I should. I just *shall!*"

Then came an explosion the like of which the Prince hoped he would never hear again. A thousand colours flared around him, the earth shook, rocks cracked to pieces and a gale-force wind swept everything away.

When the Prince opened his eyes again, the valley was being washed with warm clear afternoon light, and every blade of grass was edged with gold. Not a trace of anything dark remained, but then he'd known it would be gone, gone far away, back to the no-place it had come from. All around, people and animals were milling and laughing, throwing bucket helmets in the air. Many oak trees lay toppled on the ground, the rest had apparently fled. Only one sapling stood a few feet away, the sapling that had belonged to the Honnerdrin child. The Prince looked up at it, and it was lifeless and withered, killed as the child had been when it had rebelled against Nulgrave. Even so, there was a curious look about it – as if it had had the last laugh against them all, and was still somehow laughing.

The Prince put his hand on the thin trunk, and swore a promise, occasionally wiping his eyes.

CHAPTER SEVENTEEN

The Secret

It was twilight before the Prince could get away from the Victory Feast.

Eventually he slipped out in the middle of the one hundred and third toast, mounted the horse, and rode away up the hills to the place where Vultikan's bonfire still burned. It was a fine clear night, and stars were coming out, and every so often a silver flower-chariot would gallop by overhead, full of people singing sweet, strange, joyful songs.

Up on the hillock stood Gemael the Red, just as they had had to leave her. Her eyes darted at the Prince.

"We won," said he. "Didn't we, horse?"

"Naturally," said the horse.

The Prince got down and went up the hillock. When he was in front of Gemael he spun round the other way on his foot and said, "Pellepor-in-Zarrazax."

Gemael gave a small scream, waved her arms and ran up and hugged him.

"However did you do it? I thought only the Witch could make it work."

"I expect it's because I'm the Looked-for Deliverer," said the Prince. "Or there may be some even sillier reason. You know what it's like here."

The three moons rose together over the hills.

"They don't usually come all at once," said the horse.

"Perhaps they're celebrating too," said the Prince.

He sat himself and Gemael on the hillside while the horse changed into a lion and went to roll in some ferns.

"I know who I am now," said the Prince.

"Yes. I guessed you did. So I suppose you'll be going back to – wherever it is. Where is it, actually?"

"It's a place with one moon and a very hot sun, with lots of buildings, and roads with things that run up and down on them and are called cars and buses. Everything there makes sense, and it's rather boring."

"How did you get here?" asked Gemael. "And *who* are you?"

"No one special," he said. "Certainly not a prince. I was very poor and very old, and had nothing and no one. As to how I got here. Well." The Prince smiled. "I remember the first thing I thought of in the Waste was an acorn."

"An *acorn*?"

"Yes. And no wonder. I was sheltering from the rain under an oak tree – not a Honnerdrin tree, there's nothing like that where *I* come from – and an acorn fell on my head from a great height. I expect you know that if something small falls a long way it becomes very dangerous when it hits you. And it was *very* dangerous. I'm afraid that that acorn finished me off in my world, so I *can't* go back, even if I wanted to. Which I don't," he added. "Something pushed me right out of one world into another. And this world is a challenge. Look at all the bare ground and the dead trees and the wastes. Someone needs to plant things and build things – besides, I promised a friend I'd do my best. We'll have to give it a name. How about Threemoon?"

"Threemoon," echoed Gemael disapprovingly.

"And it really is the back of beyond," smiled the Prince wistfully, "and in a way we *are* on its back, aren't we? Its stone bones show through a lot, and it hasn't much fur, though the horse is rolling in some now – fern fur."

Gemael clicked her tongue, so the Prince said quickly, "Tell me, Gemael, if I built you a palace, would you come and live with me in it, and be Lady of that instead of Lady of the Waste?"

Gemael had never been one for not speaking her mind.

"Yes," she said promptly. "A very good idea."

They stared up at the daisy-white stars and down at the horse-lion rolling on its back below them.

"Tell us a story, horse," said the Prince dreamily.

"Once upon a time— " began the horse.

The Prince interrupted, "Sorry. I forgot. You can't talk, can you?"

In the middle of the night Gemant the Red felt a terrible urge to ride off over the hills of Threemoon. He buckled on his magic sword, jumped on his coal-black horse, and did so.

As dawn was breaking he came to a barren rocky place. On a rock a large, evil-looking bird, with black eyes, was preening itself with a hooked red beak.

"Oh, er—" said Gemant, feeling he'd seen the bird somewhere before.

"She's in there," said the bird, jerking one wing at a small cave nearby. "If you want her."

156

Gemant got off the horse and went into the cave.

A beautiful girl, with long fair hair and a ragged yellow dress, was sitting in one corner. At her feet crouched a black furry thing with a tail, which Gemant recognised as a Bozzle, and a grey snaky thing with two heads, which was a Bazzle.

"Sir Knight," whispered the beautiful girl, "I throw myself on your mercy."

The Bozzle and the Bazzle leered at each other.

Gemant squared his shoulders.

"I'll look after you, Ysome," he said firmly, "as long as you do as you're told."

"Yes, Gemant," said Ysome the Saffron meekly, and put her hand in his.

"Out!" roared Gemant to the Bozzle and the Bazzle, and they fled. "Off with you!" shouted Gemant at the evil-looking bird, which flapped up into the sky along with three or four Oggrings that had been hanging around hopefully on the rocks.

Gemant mounted Ysome before him on his horse, and rode with her back towards the Victory Camp. They only stopped once, shortly after Ysome had started to practise spells and mutter about bone castles and dragons, and then it wasn't for long. Just long enough, in fact, for Gemant to bellow her into astonished total silence.

BEAVER BOOKS FOR OLDER READERS

There are loads of exciting books for older readers in Beaver. They are available in bookshops or they can be ordered directly from us. Just complete the form below and send the right amount of money and the books will be sent to you at home.

☐	THE RUNAWAYS	Ruth Thomas	£1.99
☐	COMPANIONS ON THE ROAD	Tanith Lee	£1.99
☐	THE GOOSEBERRY	Joan Lingard	£1.95
☐	IN THE GRIP OF WINTER	Colin Dann	£2.50
☐	THE TEMPEST TWINS Books 1 – 6	John Harvey	£1.99
☐	YOUR FRIEND, REBECCA	Linda Hoy	£1.99
☐	THE TIME OF THE GHOST	Diana Wynne Jones	£1.95
☐	WATER LANE	Tom Aitken	£1.95
☐	ALANNA	Tamora Pierce	£2.50
☐	REDWALL	Brian Jacques	£2.95
☐	BUT JASPER CAME INSTEAD	Christine Nostlinger	£1.95
☐	A BOTTLED CHERRY ANGEL	Jean Ure	£1.99
☐	A HAWK IN SILVER	Mary Gentle	£1.99
☐	WHITE FANG	Jack London	£1.95
☐	FANGS OF THE WEREWOLF	John Halkin	£1.95

If you would like to order books, please send this form, and the money due to:
ARROW BOOKS, BOOKSERVICE BY POST, PO BOX 29, DOUGLAS, ISLE OF MAN, BRITISH ISLES. Please enclose a cheque or postal order made out to Arrow Books Ltd for the amount due including 22p per book for postage and packing both for orders within the UK and for overseas orders.

NAME ....

ADDRESS ....

....

Please print clearly.

Whilst every effort is made to keep prices low it is sometimes necessary to increase cover prices at short notice. Arrow Books reserve the right to show new retail prices on covers which may differ from those previously advertised in the text or elsewhere.

BEAVER BESTSELLERS

You'll find books for everyone to enjoy from Beaver's bestselling range—there are hilarious joke books, gripping reads, wonderful stories, exciting poems and fun activity books. They are available in bookshops or they can be ordered directly from us. Just complete the form below and send the right amount of money and the books will be sent to you at home.

☐ THE ADVENTURES OF KING ROLLO	David McKee	£2.50
☐ MR PINK-WHISTLE STORIES	Enid Blyton	£1.95
☐ FOLK OF THE FARAWAY TREE	Enid Blyton	£1.99
☐ REDWALL	Brian Jacques	£2.95
☐ STRANGERS IN THE HOUSE	Joan Lingard	£1.95
☐ THE RAM OF SWEETRIVER	Colin Dann	£2.50
☐ BAD BOYES	Jim and Duncan Eldridge	£1.95
☐ ANIMAL VERSE	Raymond Wilson	£1.99
☐ A JUMBLE OF JUNGLY JOKES	John Hegarty	£1.50
☐ THE RETURN OF THE ELEPHANT JOKE BOOK	Katie Wales	£1.50
☐ THE REVENGE OF THE BRAIN SHARPENERS	Philip Curtis	£1.50
☐ THE RUNAWAYS	Ruth Thomas	£1.99
☐ EAST OF MIDNIGHT	Tanith Lee	£1.99
☐ THE BARLEY SUGAR GHOST	Hazel Townson	£1.50
☐ CRAZY COOKING	Juliet Bawden	£2.25

If you would like to order books, please send this form, and the money due to:
ARROW BOOKS, BOOKSERVICE BY POST, PO BOX 29, DOUGLAS, ISLE OF MAN, BRITISH ISLES. Please enclose a cheque or postal order made out to Arrow Books Ltd for the amount due including 22p per book for postage and packing both for orders within the UK and for overseas orders.

NAME ....

ADDRESS ....

....

Please print clearly.

Whilst every effort is made to keep prices low it is sometimes necessary to increase cover prices at short notice. Arrow Books reserve the right to show new retail prices on covers which may differ from those previously advertised in the text or elsewhere.